# These Convergent Stars

Janine A. Southard

Cover by Mae I Design
Editing by Taryn Albright
Copyediting by Rachel Lynn Solomon
Published by Martian Cantina, an imprint of Cantina Publishing

ISBN: 978-1-63327-019-0

The font used in this printing is Charter ITC Pro.

# Acknowledgements

Gigantic thanks go out to my Kickstarter backers. Without your support, *These Convergent Stars* would not be the story it is today. Thank you for believing in this novella. In particular, I'd like to thank the following backers for their contributions (in alphabetical order by first name because you have to order things somehow):

Aaron Giddings
Alan S.
Anonymous
Asti
Bob Bauman
Christopher Broussard
Crissa Doeppke
Don, Beth,
    & Meghan Ferris

Ivan
James W. Truher
Janet Armentani
Jess Downs
Mandy Wultsch
Melissa
Melissa Pagonis
Michael Baker
Miriah Hetherington

Rachel Lynn Solomon          Sifi Fan
Owens                        SwordFire
Ravi Mantena


And, of course, special thanks to Jeremy Barton, my "main investor" and spouse... who read this book in multiple iterations.

# Chapter One

*Never go looking for trouble. It'll find you.*
*– Mahdan first class Maya Qaitra's mother*

**I hereby declare this inquiry open. This is the first testimony from the ship's Mahdan. For the record, please state your full name and rank.**

Maya Qaitra. Mahdan, first class.

**All present will keep in mind this is an inquiry, not a trial. Weapons were discharged on alien soil, against standard first contact peace protocols. We will now determine all events leading up to that action.**

Do we really have to do this, commander? You were there for the tail end of it.

**And *only* for the end of it. We got involved in a *civil war*, Qaitra. Regardless of how it turned out, we have procedures, and I've got to make a**

**report about the fool thing. So just hurry up and tell the story so you can go home.**

I don't have a home, sir. Earth blew up three hundred years ago, and I just got assigned to this ship a few years back. Do you think I'll have a home someday?

**Don't be obtuse.**

Sorry, Commander Yogifire.

**No you're not. Don't lie, either. We're on the record.**

Yes, ma'am.

**So, tell me about the day you met the aliens. Start at the beginning.**

Well, I woke up in my harness....

Our transport rattled me around in my zero-g harness as we attempted to dock with the E-Tee space station. We might have standard-sized Terran docking gear, but that means nothing these days. Terran-made goods are a scarce resource in low demand. If we hadn't been Terrans ourselves—of various flavors—you can bet we'd use something else.

Now, think about this for a minute. I was floating in zero-g, sleeping untethered by gravity. I'd chosen a light harness for my sleepbox, enough to keep me from flying off into the lurking bulkheads. After a few hours of bumping around when the ship went one way and inertia took me another, I wasn't going to notice one more bump against the harness.

But when we docked with that station, I got more than a gentle nudge. Not because of the pilot, don't get me wrong. No, the problem came from the way I'd managed twist my safety belt so hard it tried to choke me. Sadly, I'd managed to turn myself around like this more than once before.

I transformed into my leonine form immediately, hands squaring into paws and arm muscles lengthening. My breasts flattened against my rib cage, my throat curved into a C. I poised claws over the harness belt closest to my face. Except... I was already in deep with the Quartermaster. Last time I'd cut myself out, he'd vowed finality. Actually, it went like this:

> Me (Mahdan first class Maya Qaitra): (sheepishly) Um.
>
> Quartermaster: (not happy) What've you done now, slitty?
>
> —Note: I let him get away with calling me *slitty* because he was justifiably mad. But I still narrowed my unmistakable, slitted cat eyes at the slur.—
>
> Me: You know how two weeks ago, ship-time, I got all tangled up in my sleeping harness and used my claws to get out?
>
> Quartermaster: (exceedingly not happy) You did it again, didn't you? This makes

number five. Y'know, our last Mahdan didn't cause problems like that.

—Note: Their last Mahdan was the most boring old lady ever. She'd been in the service long enough to make S-class, but that was pure seniority. If she'd found ten viable worlds to seed in her entire life, I'd eat my zero-g harness. The one I'm still stuck in, and that would be really irreparable.—

*Me*: I'm really sorry.

*Quartermaster*: Fine. I'll send my kids up with a new one, but this is the absolute last time!


Much as I'd prefer to avoid trouble with the Quartermaster, this harness was a fluffin' Gordian Knot, and good old Alexander created a precedent for that. And I, like Alexander, had better things to do. Like get breakfast before we finished docking.

A few quick slashes through the fraying mesh weave—I keep these babies sharp—and I was free. I could talk to the Quartermaster *after* our rest stop. Hopefully he'd be too hungover to remember that he'd sworn to leave me in permanent free fall if I ever destroyed his precious resources again. Trouble successfully deferred.

I shifted back out of my leonine form before I got to the doorway of my sleeping cell. Transforming in zero-g is *the best.* No gravity to pull your spine out of alignment when you go from four legs to two. Nope, you can just articulate through the vertebrae, like a comfortable stretch. Now hominid, I splayed my fingers all the way out and fisted them again. Fingers take some getting used to after you've been leonine.

Sure, I could've stayed in my fingerless form a while longer. I spent so much time in it those days that it felt more normal than my hominid form. Plus, a tail and a feline center of balance *do* help a lady maneuver through zero-g hallways... but they also lead to one's tail being pulled by prankster shipmates. There is nothing funny about pulling a cat's tail. Nothing.

"White stars and black space!" I caroled to my fellows on third watch when I entered the restaurant. They used to call it *the mess,* but when I first got assigned to this ship, I couldn't resist. You can't call a place a *mess* and then not make one! Food flying everywhere, tables overturned, chefs with storage bins on their heads. My company commander learned right quick the importance of calling things by proper names.

"Green grass and cool water," Simpson replied. At least *someone* had learned that planets were more my thing than ships and stations. Simpson was an apprentice pilot, and everyone knows pilots are crazy. Crazy enough to befriend the only *creepy shapeshifter* on the ship.

I grabbed a cereal sphere and filled it with kibble. Trust me, the dry cat food is the most edible thing at the restaurant. Sometimes my shipmates tried to steal it, and the cook had been known to mash it up for side dishes. I was just the only one who didn't have to sneak it.

I glided to join Simpson and resisted the urge to toss kibble at him. After all, the restaurant wasn't a *mess* anymore. Before I could convince myself that swatting my breakfast made me a benevolent Mahdan—one who shared her breakfast with those unfortunates forced to eat scrambled protein and cardboard carbohydrates—Commander Asti Yogifire's voice came over the PA.

"All right, everybody. We're safely docked and I want you all to take some off-ship rest. We'll be here for a week. Work out among yerselves who's gonna stay with the ship to watch our cargo." Crackling silence. "Except Mahdan Qaitra. You go out and meet people, figure out where we're goin' next. I don't wanna hear from you till it's time to bounce." Momentary pause. "Well? What're you waitin' for? Hop to it!" Muttered, but clearly heard: "Disgraces to the service."

Simpson grinned at me. "Off you stalk then. Scat, little kitten."

I transformed, professionally quick, and flicked a blond paw at his breakfast. His grin broadened as he pulled it out of my reach, and I retaliated with a hiss and a leap—careful to keep my claws sheathed and my rotation slow—that flipped the pair of us over and over through the air in mock-wrestle.

As we rolled toward the door, I positioned myself to sail out of the restaurant, saucy tail shake in my wake. Third watch laughed behind me, amusement flowing more freely now that I was gone.

\* \* \* \*

So my shipmates were all on *shore leave*—as some of the Navy wannabes would call it, not that there's any water in space—but not me. You heard the commander. I was here to work. It was time to sniff out all the biologically compatible E-Tees so we could send a first contact team to their planet. A team which, of course, would be us. Where else would we find Terran sort-of diplomats in this section of the universe? In *any* section of the universe?

See, after Earth got exploded, the docs engineered Baastet's Children—such a pompous name they gave us, too—to sniff out biological compatibility. Each Mahdan plays Geiger counter for a team to make sure we find suitable aliens for mating. Making sure our species could continue to survive. Procreative roulette was a luxury for *other* species, not for Terrans anymore.

I planned to start with one of the station bars. No patrons there would mind if I approached their tables, chatted them up, and maybe sniffed them a bit. I'd have preferred to go down to one of the planets this station served, but I'd have a more diverse species pool up here. I went planetside less often than I'd like, but there were perks. Who passes up a chance to have a nip on the company dollar?

But like Mama always said, I never have to go looking for trouble. Trouble finds me. Case in point: before I made it to the likely bar I'd noted in the station directory, a kitten came dashing down the empty hallway, straight for me. I know what you're thinking,

"Awww, how cute! A kitten! With its cute little blond paws and tiny little ears!" Insert vapid cooing here.

Now, usually I'd agree. I like kittens. Someday, I might even find a place to settle down and have my own. But this moment was not *someday*. I'd seen what happened to kittens on stations before:

When I was six and a cub myself, some of my littermates and I took a field trip to a local station. It was supposed to be educational. Y'know, feel the difference in synthetic air and the lightness of the gravity, et cetera. The month before, we'd visited a jungle planet to jump into exceedingly tall trees and understand humidity.

So there we were, a class of children curiously poking about—I remember ripping up some of the carpeting to tap my fingers against the metal floor beneath—when one of my classmates freaked out. To this day, I have no idea why, but that was the point of the field trips, to make sure we were comfortable with any environment. It could've been the recycled air, or being so far away from home, or a case of the flu that suddenly came on, but whatever the reason, she shifted.

Now, remember, she was only five or six, so she couldn't become a huge, fearsome lion. One second she was a little girl in a school uniform, and the next second her space was occupied by a black cub, no bigger than a small housecat. One of the other girls in our class threw a sparkly ball a short ways down the hallway—we all carried toys—and the cub ran after it, and straight into four drunken men.

This was a heavily Terran-populated station—at least 30 percent—so a drunkard recognized the cat for one of Baastet's Children, rather than an actual animal. "Baastard freak!" he screeched. "You should be put down like the rest of your slutty kind!"

Then he stepped on her so hard that her neck broke. None of us cried out. The chaperones made sure of that. Probably saved our lives.

Right, where was I? So there's this kitten dashing down the hallway toward me. No way was I going to leave it to fend for itself. Not even if it turned out to be an actual feline, rather than one of my far-flung kin. She'd just have to come along, and I'd tell the commander she was my pet or my apprentice or something. If I never found her family, our ship could use a second shapeshifter, a Mahdan-in-training.

As she closed in and moved to pass me, I scooped her up. No tag. Definitely one of Baastet's Children, then. Even if she did smell a little odd. And what was one of us doing all on her lonesome way out here? We were farther out from the old, exploded homestead than any ship had ever been. Or so I'd thought.

Not important now. "Hush, little one," I whispered and transformed a hand so that she could understand I was like her. "I won't let anyone hurt you. We'll find your parents soon."

The muddy sound of multiple shoes thudding along and the singing of completely unintelligible songs meant that some drunken idiots were coming my way. And as we know, drunken idiots are often dangerous idiots, stationside. Fluffing fluff! I prepared to shift. I'd made a promise, and no kittens were getting killed on my watch.

I cuddled the kitten against my chest and schooled my breathing. No reason for those boys to give us a second glance. Nope. They could just pass us by. Still, I tensed my shoulders and loosened the mental muscles that held my body hominid. I waited in readiness, holding a slightly squirming kitten, hoping absolutely nothing was going to happen.

Things never turn out like you hope.

# Chapter Two

*Really, child! Stop being so melodramatic.*
*– Zean Skyline's mom*

**TESTIMONY ENTERED INTO RECORD.**

**From the deposition of Zean Skyline (alien, Elsajh native).**

**Courtesy of the Elsajh Protectors' Office.**

*Ten hours earlier*

Warm breezes swept grass seed and plains dust over Zean's skin. She faced off with her lifelong nemeses in her parents' wildflower garden.

"Zean and Rzis, traveling over the plain, how many babes before she comes home again?" chanted her eldest brother, the obnoxious twit. Babies? Not if she could help it. Mum and Da weren't going to force her to marry this guy, were they? They'd always said she'd have veto power over her fiancé after she finished school, so long as she *did* choose a partner of Skyline descent before her potential breeding years ended.

Then again, maybe they'd changed their minds. After all, she'd dropped out of school, with all its frustrating business and deportment classes. At least the dance classes had been useful. Nowadays, she taught a mean burlesque on the other side of town, where her lover lived. Zean would get around to telling Mum about the plebian-style dancing eventually. She'd already told them about her dearest Szueckr, but the family liked to pretend her non-Skyline lover was a simple phase.

"Five, six, seven, eight." Her other five brothers joined in counting her hypothetical children.

The flowers grew tall and lilac, but they could've been weeds for all Zean appreciated them. The wind in her face barely chilled her anger.

She resisted the urge to stamp her feet. Maybe it would've been okay for a few minutes, but this had been going on for hours. Apparently, her parents' Chosen was coming to visit tomorrow morning.

"Who cares that you dropped out of school, huh, Zee-zee?" poked the youngest. "You don't need smarts to get your man!"

She growled and pulled with her mind, grasping at the earth beneath her feet, at the flowers in the wildflower garden, at the sun-grayed rocks limning the path to the house. She ignored their laughter and their expectation that marrying some stranger was of the utmost importance. With a great heave on the extra mass, she shifted into her largest form yet: a pale greatcat of her own imagining, shoulder-high on her tallest brother, with pointed teeth and deadly claws. She was an intimidating predator of a kind the world had never seen. She'd always had a stellar imagination.

Rumbling louder, she swiped her right paw at the closest sibling, claws unsheathed. If he got hurt, *he* could explain to Mum how it happened. The boys scattered, and she bared her incisors in triumph before bounding up the tall tree that had a branch conveniently placed next to the window of Da's empty study.

"Zee, be careful! If you lose any of that extra mass..." warned the eldest in a voice that actually sounded concerned.

*Gee, thanks, bro.* She flicked the catch on the window. *What if I were holding this large cat together with bravado and anger, huh? What'd happen to me if I let in your little seed of doubt? Yeah, I'd lose control, and your little sister would be gone for good. All this mass reduced to dust. Lucky for you, I know what I'm doing and I'm fine.*

She grabbed some cash from the office. It'd be enough for groceries and things. They owed her that for chasing her away with their attempt to marry her off. *I'm just going to take off for a few days. Long enough to avoid this guy Mum and Da are bringing.*

She cinched a lightweight sash around her waist, its hidden pockets secreting away Da's cash and her own odds-and-evens sticks, and she was ready to scamper. She'd stay with Szueckr in their apartment for as long as she wanted this time. It was so unfair that they had to spend so many days apart! Zean bounded across town on four feet, letting the adrenaline calm her anger. Her brothers weren't *that* bad, after all, just annoying sometimes. Most of the time.

She transformed two-legged to open the door of the Sunlight Café, a place where she was the only regular patron of Skyline descent. Nobody else with her lineage would set foot in the place, no doubt. The owners kept the place very cool, an expensive proposition since the structure was an upside-down bowl made of fish-scale glass. Essentially a giant greenhouse, the café was full of seats that offered natural light.

"Zean!" called a player from the crowded table farthest from the door. "Test your luck at the sticks. You can have my place."

"If you insist." The leash she'd evaded—her unwanted fiancé and stupid brothers—melted into the past. Stick-playing required a clear mind.

"I insist," purred a player in a flesh-colored shirt. "I insist that you empty your money into my pockets. I call doubles."

Zean flipped a stick across her downy golden knuckles. Some of her tablemates had taken to discussing politics. Ugh. Apparently, a whole crew Shalanite separatists had been discovered by the Protectors' Office, and five major instigators of violence and political unrest had been taken into custody. She used the stick to clean the space between her nails and her finger pads.

Two hours later, she was up a miniscule amount and a shuttle ticket for later that afternoon. *That'll get me adequately far from my parents' latest project.*

"Oooh, Zean," a player motioned with his stick bundle, "lover-boy just walked in."

Zean shook hands with her opponents to thank them for the game and moved to meet Szueckr on the café's centerboards. He placed his stringed instruments on the floor and grabbed her in his arms, sliding a smooth hand against the base of her spine under her trousers and spinning her into the nearest table. He pushed her against the table-top and nuzzled their cheeks together to the music of catcalls.

"Hey, baby," she greeted after she'd been fully cuddled. Szueckr's ancestors were purely Elsajh stock, not a single Sky Person had dispersed genes into *that* family tree way back when. He couldn't transform into any feline forms, didn't have any of the instincts. But he'd learned how to show affection and keep her happy like any good Skyline would. No potential mate her parents found could possibly be as wonderful as Szueckr. "I was waiting for you."

He looked at the sticks in her hand. "I bet you were," he teased gently. "What's our plan today, lovely?"

They only had a couple of hours together before her stick-winnings said she had to go. She'd won herself a ticket on the shuttle to the second nearest space station.

She nuzzled his hair. "I can't, baby. I'm going away for a few days until my parents calm down. We'll reunite before you have a chance to miss me."

\* \* \* \*

Transport to and from the station was the dullest method of travel ever invented, but the old seats still had a bit of plush to them, and she'd shared a quiet car with a pair of offworlders who'd come down for the tail-end of tourist season. On arrival, she found a locker for rent and put all of her belongings in it.

Pushing out to get rid of extra mass, she shifted into a kitten. No one bothered with kittens, and fewer gawkers would recognize her tiny shape. On the off chance that her parents sent a hunting party, they'd search for something bigger. Her brothers always protested that it wasn't fair how she could be massive and they couldn't. People remembered that. They forgot she could do small too. The feline gamut as available to anyone who practiced, something they eschewed.

"The smaller bodies are enough, Zee-zee." They all seemed to feel the same. "It's not as though I need any more than that. What would I do besides get confused about who I was supposed to be? A form for playing, a form for state diplomatic functions, a form that my wife thinks is sexy... and that's probably too many."

Her brothers were idiots, of course, which was why they completely missed the beauty of other forms. She shifted to hide, shifted to threaten siblings, shifted for playtime, shifted to prove she could master any feline form real or imaginable.

Her eyes tracked a speck of dust as it fell through a beam of light, and Zean crouched low. Pounced! Of course, the dust mote dodged, and she had to follow. Tearing down mostly empty corridors, she pursued her ever-changing quarry until she suddenly found herself in a pair of warm arms.

"Hush, little one," said the arms' owner before transforming a menacing paw in front of Zean's face. "I won't let anyone hurt you. We'll find your parents soon."

Zean bunched her muscles in preparation to jump down—to change back and protest—when she heard the clatter of boots on metals flooring. Her parents' hunting party! Well, that was too bad because no one was looking for a kitten. Zean would simply stay in this shape, and her family's hired men would never be the wiser. All she had to do was stay quiet and unobtrusive.

Unfortunately, remaining in the background ceased to be an option.

The woman released Zean and shifted. Zean had thought she knew all the Skylines on Elsajh, but she'd never seen this woman, this woman who had transformed into a large blond feline similar to her favorite imaginary greatcat form.

Zean would have stuck around to chat, but she had freedom to ensure. She gave a small, parting *mew* and dashed off in the other direction.

# Chapter Three

*Never compromise your cover on a station.*
*– Mrs. Jones, Maya's third grade teacher*

**You haven't even gotten to the part about meeting people from Elsajh yet, Mahdan.**

Well, technically, I already had. I just didn't know it yet.

**Technically?**

Who's telling this story anyway?

**You're not telling a story; you're giving a statement.**

Statement, schmatement.

**Fine. So what happened next, o great and benevolent storyteller?**

I was still hoping I wouldn't have to change at this point. The drunken idiots were a few feet away from us when they started in. From the tone of things, Redheaded Idiot made an unsavory comment about Brunette Idiot, and Tall Idiot took offense on his behalf. They were speaking some non-standard language, though, so I couldn't be sure.

A neat swing-and-punch combo, and Redheaded Idiot was on the floor. He leapt to his feet and shook a fist. Brunette Idiot shushed them. Pointed at me and the kitten.

Yeah, I know the drill. Baastet's Children should never compromise their hominid cover on a station. Blend in with the rest of the hominids, play like we're normal Terrans. Good advice, but I had to forget it. No one was going to hurt a kid while I was around.

I shifted. You want a piece of this kitten? Let's see how you boys deal with a Terran lion, first. Baastet's Children might only get one cat form, but it's a blood-curling predator.

My cover? Oh so compromised.

I offered a feline smirk when they screamed, which only led to more screaming. These teeth are nothing to sneer at, unless you sneer with bigger teeth. But drunken idiots are still idiots. Here they were, faced with a huge, carnivorous predator, and what did they do? Go back to brawling with each other. Brunette Idiot fell to a kick from Redheaded Idiot which put that one closer to me.

I growled and swiped at him. Fair warning. If he got any closer, he'd be in ribbons. Too bad he took that as an invitation—or an insult to his mother—and yelled something at me. Brunette sprang forward, launching himself at my head. I sidestepped and sank my incisors into his hand. It tasted like rock candy.

Now, if we were on solid ground, I'd've done more damage. But stations look down on brawling; being the victor only means that you're a greater threat to station security. So you have to take your victims down nice-like.

Did I mention that the kitten had run off by this point? Yeah, it had. But I was embroiled in the action now. I had to keep its escape path clear.

Anyway, with Brunette's hand missing a nibble, Tall started screaming. Brunette looked at his bleeding appendage and joined in, high-pitched and whiny. They pulled at each other's clothes, no longer working to harm each other but to get away from the fluffin' massive cat in the hallway. Brunette's shirt started to unravel where Tall scrabbled at it.

A deep sniff told me what the sugary blood in my mouth already suggested. These guys were no Terrans—not even biologically compatible with us— and I'd launched to that kitten's defense for mere prov-ocation. Maybe *no* provocation. If station security tossed me in their brig, the commander'd shave my fur.

Another muddy patter of boots signaled the arrival of a four-man team. The men on the team were also dressed dissimilar to Terrans, preferring loose linen pants with neck-high shirts and bulky jackets that could hide any multitude of tricks. The obvious leader of the group waved a stick—fine, a *baton*—at Redhead, who scrambled out after his brawl-mates.

What with the crazy outfits and stick-wielding, I was pretty sure the newcomers weren't Terrans either. Oh, they looked like us. Smelled more like us than the guys who'd just left. But they weren't us. I needed a closer sniff, and maybe a taste of their blood to confirm whether this was exactly the sort of group I was supposed to track down: alien life forms who could reproduce with the remains of our species.

Unfortunately, these newcomers had met me while leonine, and nobody likes Baastet's Children on stations, as far as I know. Tolerate, sure. Want, no. And I'd never come across another species of shapeshifting kitties, so our reputation was all our own.

I watched the leader, cataloguing his features and waiting for my chance to dash. Taller than me, soft nose, pointy jaw, sienna skin. I could always go hominid and meet him later, and he'd be none the wiser. No problem, right? Except that these guys were a professional outfit and watched me back with patient equanimity.

The leader hid his hands in his bulky sleeves, making my fur shiver along my body. With his hands out of sight, he could be doing anything. Secretive types make me jumpy. Make all Terrans jumpy. Makes us wonder who the fluffin' genocidal creeps were that did in our planet and where they were hiding till they made their move.

Right, so the leader had his hands up his sleeves, all secret-like, and then he bowed to me. Bowed, like something out of a Terran Chinese drama. "I'm glad we found you, Miss Zean," he said. I was the only person in the hall, so that made me *Miss Zean.* "Your parents have been worried since they realized you were missing. Please come along."

Well. That was different. If I'd needed more proof that these guys weren't Terrans, I certainly had it. Every Terran knew big cats deserved no disrespect as either animals or Baastet's Children.

These guys were perfect for my assignment. My nose told me their species was—probably—biologically compatible with Terrans, and they already had a great relationship with cat people of some kind or another. Other cat people! This was the best fluffin' thing ever.

Unless the cat people had enslaved them, or something.

Only one way to find out: spending a couple of days with them. Question was, did I introduce myself and do this in the approved style? The way I was trained to: by approaching them as a Terran first contact specialist. Or did I let them continue to think I was this *Miss Zean*?

Hiding and pretending. These are not the Terran way. Oh, sure, we may bend the truth a little—*Colonial Seeding Team:* (sincerely) "We're just peaceful explorers; why don't we leave a few diplomats here on your planet?"—but we never lie. On the other hand, this was a prime opportunity to learn how these newcomers would treat my particular subset of the population.

All I had to do was play it cool and keep my conscience leashed. Besides, these guys were clearly dangerous—ask Redheaded Idiot—and they needed this *Miss Zean.* On the other paw, they needed *Mahdan first class Maya Qaitra* the same way they needed three ears.

All right, then. In the interests of interplanetary

unity—and not getting knocked over the head—I'd rumble along for now. I nodded at the leader and trotted docilely when he said, "Follow me." The other three team members came behind, covering my six and looking ridiculous in those loose, linen-equivalent pants.

I followed right out to the docking ring where they had a small eight-person vehicle. I cocked my head.

"Your parents were most displeased, Miss Zean," he said, as if apologizing for the vehicle. Not that it meant anything to me, but it might've to Miss Zean. "If you'll pile in the back, we'll land at Elsajh shortly."

Elsajh, huh? Is that the name of a city or a planet? I wondered how I was supposed to spell that as I curled up in the backseat and changed just my hands to the dexterous style in order to type out a short message to my company commander on my wrist tele. Sure, the commander had said he expected my silence till I wanted to leave. Well, too bad for him.

*Commander*, I typed. *Have made contact with 'Elsajh'. Have been taken off station, probably to 'Alseg' (sp?). When you figure out where I am, you probably want to come. Yours, the First Contact Specialist*

Well, the details were her problem. My duty was meeting these people, making sure they'd welcome a small group of *diplomats and scientists* who would later form a little Terra, and managing not to get killed or jailed when these guys figured out their Miss Zean was still missing. She'd be fine wherever she was, I hoped. Her troubles sounded like the kind that growing up would fix.

# Chapter Four

*Your functions are to observe and protect.*
*– Elsajh Protectors' Office manual, page 1*

**TESTIMONY ENTERED INTO RECORD.**

**From the deposition of Rzis Skyline (alien, Elsajh native).**

**Courtesy of the Elsajh Protectors' Office.**

Some invisible creature wanted to get out of Rzis's innards, preferably through his throat. He swallowed down bile in an ongoing effort to drown the monster of nervousness. This first meeting with his would-be bride was already going wrong. He vibrated with the same nervousness his coworkers talked about when they ran into a hostage situation. All this waiting took a toll!

He'd worked hard to reach his position with the Protectors' Office, often at the expense of his personal life, and now he was ready to think about next steps. At home, he was a bit lonely. At work, he needed to project competence in all things, but he was approaching the age where a Skyline was judged on the lineage of his offspring. He'd make some Skyline lady happy someday, but it looked less and less like that potential lady would be Zean.

He tried to project his *calm and in control* persona to Zean's parents while they shared glasses of juice in the family's receiving parlor. They'd discussed Zean's hobbies, his personal involvement in apprehending a major Shalanite cell, and when the family expected grandchildren. All things much better discussed with his intended herself.

He suspected that the conversation with her would go maybe half as well. Her parents clearly wanted the match—they'd approached *him*, after all, with their interest and their political influence—but the daughter couldn't even be bothered to show up. Plus, her mother's dappled hands shook with every pour of juice, and the couple kept looking toward the door.

And then she was there, escorted by an honor guard. Her parents rocketed from their sofa and practically stampeded to the door to usher their girl inside *and probably to make sure she doesn't escape*, he thought with an uncharitable smirk.

For her sake, he was thankful for his own presence. No parent scolded a child in front of a potential match. Regardless of the undisclosed fact that he'd decided to step aside. Yes, this match would have been great for his reputation and for his children's futures, but he had no intention of tying himself to someone who wished to reject him. Someone willful and resourceful, yes. Someone who saw him as unwelcome, no.

The honor guard left the room, providing an unobstructed view, and Rzis considered his would-be bride. She appeared as a large cat of a type he'd never seen before, blonde and sleek, chest height, with a predator's eyes and teeth. Probably with sharp claws as well. Zean's brothers had whispered that his intended was the most talented at pulling in extra mass to make whole multitudes of larger forms, and those whispers were proving true.

His heart slowed as his respect ratcheted up. Usually, people who met him wanted to be judged as small and in need of his aid. As part of the Protectors' Office, protection was his job, and strangers seemed to hope that predilection would carry into his off-hours. It did, actually, but he'd prefer to avoid the obligation. Zean, though... In this form, she might be able to take him down and run off before he had the chance to transform.

If this meeting hadn't been bungled so badly by the family, he and Zean might have been friends. As it was, this was going to be one of *those* dates. The kind where everyone wanted to go home, but nobody could scamper off without causing a hiss.

Moments passed. Zean remained stubbornly in this large cat form, no matter the number of admonishments from a mother whose downy face was turning red even through her mottled natural camouflage.

Politeness dictated his correct course of action.

Rzis tugged on the air particles and the wood in the

fireplace—making an effort not to pull on the rug beneath his feet, nor the ornate table on which his juice glass sat; there was a reason his father had beaten him for transforming indoors as a child—and shifted to match her. He purred with pride at the accomplishment, since very few Skylines bothered to master a large form. His own fur was pure black on a predator's body with a sleek runner's build. His newly sharpened silver eyes could see every detail from leagues away.

Sniffing hard with his freshly sensitized nose, he tried to distinguish the dynamics of the situation. As expected, the parents exuded nerves and the sour scent of despairing anticipation, to match their fidgeting and rapid heartbeats. Zean, however, was different.

Rzis had expected the sharp scent-taste of rage. He had also expected her to snap at her family in pique. But Zean, like him, was taking in details with her yellow-green eyes, smelling the emotions in the air. She seemed curious about her own parents, as if this entire situation was a surprise and she needed to divine all parties' motivations.

That was just classic. It seemed as though nobody had even bothered to tell her that he'd be visiting today. Here he'd resigned himself to her disinterest and readied himself to move on, when it turned out that there was still a slim chance that he ought to press his suit. Or at least to say, "Hi."

Zean's parents looked at him. "Go ahead," encouraged her mother. "Greet your bride-to-be."

Zean's whole body tensed, and she focused her full attention on Rzis. With her eyes trained on him and his movements, she relaxed muscle by muscle, one at a time. That deliberate relaxation heralded a constant readiness. He wished some of the newbies at the Protectors' Office had that level of discipline and concentration, especially when dealing with Shalanite insurgents... or offworlder tourists.

Ever so slowly, he edged toward her, making sure to telegraph his intentions. At half a body's length away, he stretched his neck forward to offer his nose and cheeks for mutual sniffing and—potentially—rubbing, the classic Skyline greeting, depending on how tactile both parties were. This was the only part of this meeting proceeding in a normal manner, a simple meet-and-greet.

She came to life. Relaxed muscles surged, propelling her forward. The force behind her nudge, from his head to shoulder to haunch, nearly pushed him over. No need to play tentative here. On her next pass, he matched her for pressure and movement.

Zean's mother clasped her hands to her chest. "It's so good to see youngsters getting along," she cooed. "We'll leave you two alone. Zee-zee, why don't you take Rzis out for a walk in the wildflower garden?" Anyone with a pushy parent could tell this was more an order than a suggestion. If things went well, he'd be part of this family, and the woman would be *his* pushy parent.

Left alone and with the greetings completed, the pair fidgeted side by side, looking off in various directions.

Here was the fireplace: devoid of wood.

Here was the table: with empty juice glasses on it.

Here was the door: through which Zean had been dragged.

Zean maintained her greatcat form and made no move to shift. On the one paw, this saved him from making silly small talk. On the other paw, what should they do other than stand here awkwardly? His intestinal monster made another bid from freedom. Again, he swallowed the nervousness down. Her standing at his side was a positive omen, but the silence detracted.

Getting outside into the fresh air might solve all their immediate problems, including pleasing her mother. Rzis made a motion toward the door, but was stopped by a sub-vocal growl. He pulled up sharply and chanced a look at the predator beside him. What had he done wrong?

The blond cat nipped gently at his shoulder in a sign to follow, an *intimate* sign to follow. This was good. When she jumped to the window sill and unlocked the pane with a deft *snickt* of her claws, he revised that thought: this was marvelous.

Silent and controlled, they slipped out the window and into the wildflower garden, as Zean's mother had *suggested*. They shimmied down to the ground, and the blonde leapt.

*Attack!*

They rolled sideways in the tall grass, and he managed to keep his claws pulled in. It wouldn't be polite to harm one's intended—and hostess—no matter the provocation. A good thing, too. The blonde quickly got the advantage, but never pressed it, simply nipping his nose, shoulder, throat before springing off to start the fight again. No one's claws ventured out play.

Not an attack, then, but a game. She'd keep him on his toes for certain. He bared his long, curved teeth in a predatory smile and threw himself into the play, hurtling full speed into her body and tumbling both of them to the ground.

They skidded and rolled in the dirt before springing apart, ears cocked to identify what had disturbed them. Zean must have figured it out first, because Rzis felt the gentle nudge of her forehead against the underside of his chin, the soft tap guiding him to look left through a small copse of plush trees.

In a clearing, Zean's six brothers whooped to get their attention. One made kissing noises, and two others pretended to be cats—without having shifted—who were fighting and then making up over and over. A fourth brother started in on the school yard refrain: "Rzis and Zean, traveling over the plain, how many babes before she comes home again?"

Zean shot Rzis a look that said, *And you want to marry into this?* Then she nodded up at the trees to her right and made a circular wag with her tail. Oh yes. This was his kind of woman—prepared, a planner, and perfectly able to take care of herself.

As directed, he leapt upward onto the lowest tree branches and crept around the clearing at that height. He snuck behind the boys, while the six brothers single-tracked on lonely Zean.

One of the play fighters started to make baby noises. "Awwww. Poor Zee-zee! All by your lonesome without your big, strong fiancé to protect you. Did he dump you, little baby?"

Zean growled so Rzis could hear her, a clear signal to strike. As she vaulted forward—teeth and claws bared—Rzis padded down the tree on the other side of the clearing and matched her roar.

With careful swipes that barely grazed their victims, the pair quickly made the boys scatter. Three of the boys transformed into cats—barely hip-high, using exactly their own mass for the transformations—in order to escape faster.

They let their prey depart. Once the clearing was as devoid of boys as it was of trees, they settled down to the grass to enjoy their victory, chuffing little laughs at their adversaries' fates.

They lazed on the ground, and Rzis reveled in the sunshine, the games, the playfully aggressive company. Was she ready to talk to him, to build a friendship based on more than athletics and body language?

Rzis was tempted to transform to his two-legged form, to push the issue. But he wasn't sure. If she were ready for such a thing, she'd initiate it herself. Unless she believed she'd proven her independence and preferred to force him into the more dominant role going forward.

He hadn't collected enough facts to know.

The transformation situation was taken out of his hands. A high pitched whine reverberated against his overly sensitive ears, and he shifted out of cat form to dampen the noise. "Rzis here," he answered the Urgent Summons.

The response came from the Protectors' Office through further vibrations. It looked as though he'd have to cut off this pleasant excursion, after all. At the beginning of the afternoon, he'd have welcomed the excuse to scamper, but now he was reluctant to leave. Still, he had a job to do. He was a Protector above all, and from his current location he'd be first on the scene.

He pressed his hands against the opposite forearms, in front of his chest, and bowed deeply. "Zean, I'm sorry to cut short our afternoon, but I can't be choosy about the fate and freedom of my protectorate." He took refuge in the standard phrases of his department. Still, he wouldn't want her to think he'd abandon her for something unimportant. "There's a Shalanite attempting to annex a bank downtown, on a very busy block, and I have to be there before he kills someone."

He bowed again, and transformed to race to the public area. He heard a rustling behind him, so perhaps she had turned around and headed home. Or transformed to watch him with different eyes? Or—

No. He excised those thoughts. No use speculating on her actions and motivations. Not until he knew more about her.

He hoped he'd be allowed to visit her again.

# Chapter Five

*Ye Shalanites constrained / our world we will
regain.*
*– Elsajh folk song*

**Aha! The Shalanites. I'd wondered when they
were going to show up. Is this when you told the
representative from the Protector's Office your
true identity in exchange for information about
this violent faction?**

Nope.

**Why the bloody hell not?**

I didn't really have the time, ma'am. Besides, I continued the investigation without having to trade any
information. It's my job. I have discretion in the field.

**So, if the Protector didn't tell you, how did you
learn enough about the Shalanites that you felt**

comfortable embroiling us all in a civil war with them? A "terrorist action"? I still don't know what to call it.

I padded along behind Rzis, down dusty streets and through cozy alleys bordered by a perplexing mix of delicate new construction and pitted stone walls that had clearly stood against the tossings of time and weather. I kept far enough behind that he wouldn't mark me.

How better to research a new world than by following the local law to the scene of some really weird sounding crime? As ship's Mahdan—and, thus, first contact specialist—I heard plenty of strange terms, so the perp's being "a Shalanite" was no problem. But this crime matched nothing I'd heard of before. How did small-time guys annex anything? And who would bother to annex a bank?

Once I learned the answers, maybe I'd suggest to the commander that we bypass this world entirely.

I kept expecting shouts and complaints. My mind created an echo here—*Baastards should all be put down!*—and another over there—*Goodness! Look at those teeth!*. I bared my incisors at this imagined detractor. Why did they always point out the teeth, as if mentioning them stopped me from using them?

But it didn't go down like that. No one shouted at all. A few people cleared out of our path, yes, but we were heavy things barreling along. Also, my unwitting companion was The Law. If anyone recognized him, they'd scamper away for that reason alone.

When we reached the bank, Rzis was the first enforcer on location, so he had to distinguish the facts and stall till his pack arrived. The guy inside the bank, however, had me fluffin' flummoxed.

Think about it for a minute. You're holding up a bank. What are you there for? Money. Otherwise, why bother with the bank? Okay, your other reason could be to keep others from said money, on the assumption that banks are unconnected. In that second case, you could more effectively blow the place up, preferably with something that makes fiat money impossible to repair.

So, there're a couple of plans and motives. But all they had in common with reality was the location. There was a guy holding up a bank. He had hostages, but made no fuss about killing anyone. No ransom note on hand. His pockets could maybe carry a double handful of precious whatever.

Over a primitive loudspeaker he repeated, "I annex this bank and the property on which it stands for the state of Shalal. All Shalanite citizens are welcome here. I annex this bank..." And so on in perpetual duplication.

Rzis shifted hominid about twenty feet from the bank's front door. I hadn't paid him much attention earlier, before he'd gone leonine, but now I could see that he was quite the strapping young lad. He was about six-foot-four—a sensible for the size considering his other form—though he looked older than I'd thought he'd be. Maybe he'd waited till he was successful before embroiling himself in the arranged-marriage market.

He had the same dark coloring and shiny hair as his leonine self, and that shiny hair included a gentle dusting across his face and arms. Where a Terran would have nearly invisible vellus hair, he had a dark, downy, not-quite-fur. Aliens. What can you do? I wanted to pet him.

Come to think of it, Zean's parents might have had the same extra fuzziness. But their paler coloration meant I hadn't noticed. I'd have to keep an eye out.

I slunk behind one of the velvety lilac trees—a texture and color combination particular to this world—and transformed back to hominid. This would be the perfect chance to talk to someone uninvolved with my little identity crisis. I wasn't worried about bad reactions to foreigners. This planet had plenty of offworld visitors that I'd seen. And no one could mistake my skintight uniform for anything other than *foreign*, not with the way these guys hid their bodies and their belongings.

I don't know how things work for every shapeshifter in the universe, but Baastet's Children keep our clothes from form to form. A medic had once tried to describe it as a surface area thing, that your body considers the clothing part of you if there's enough touching skin, but I wasn't an expert. Could be true. Could be not. The important part was that I'd come down to this planet wearing a set of Terran clothes, and I was still wearing them.

I slipped on my sunglasses to hide my slitted pupils. I could only hope for so many concessions made for my foreignness, and my eyes would *really* stand out. On two legs, I casually ambled over to a group of three bank-facing gawkers. "This happen a lot around here?" Curiosity about potential new allies was my job.

One of the rubberneckers *shush*ed me, but another—two-thirds my height and sporting pink hair that I'd love to make a toy out of—bowed. They did a lot of bowing on this planet. "Not too often. The Shalanites like to pretend they have a country and annex land for it." My informant didn't have the lush hair that dusted Rzis's hominid body. It made her look more Terran. Less alien. "The Protectors will keep us all safe. Don't worry. Shalanites've never killed an offworlder. Have you been enjoying your visit?"

I thought I understood the set-up as she explained it. The man inside believed he was fighting a civil war, but the ruling party referred to him as a *terrorist* rather than a *freedom fighter* or even an *enemy combatant*. Also important, the supposed terrorist group had thus far refrained from harming uninvolved parties, like tourists. "Why don't they have a country?"

My informer shook her head in sympathy, the kind of sympathy you spare for the mentally deficient who can't help themselves. Some people treated Baastet's Children with that sort of sympathy, since we were *made* and not *volunteers*. People could be stupid. "Well, there aren't really separate countries here on Elsajh. But they want to return to the old ways, no matter what they have to do to get them back."

Anti-progress. Okay, maybe the Shalanites *were* bad guys, at least as far as interacting and interbreeding with other species was concerned. I tilted my head to the side encouragingly, a catlike gesture I hoped translated on this cat-happy world. "The old ways?"

"Before the Sky People came."

My eyes rolled, thankfully hidden. Right. Of course. So helpful. I readjusted my sunglasses. "When was that?"

She shrugged, almost Gallic. Yes, our peoples had much in common. "Three, four thousand years ago. They helped us out of our warlike fugue state, lived among us, had children with us, and then disappeared."

Behind us, Rzis opened lines of communication with the self-proclaimed Shalanite. "This is Rzis Skyline with the Protectors' Office," he called. "Come out of the bank with your weapons unpowered, and you may be granted leniency by the Court."

Clearly, this was one of those universal things. Law enforcement had to let the bad guys give themselves up, not that they ever did. Has anyone ever changed their mind at this point? The comment about *unpowered* weapons was a positive observation for my ever-expanding file, indicating a level of technology maybe comparable to ours. The commander'd be happy to hear it. Though, before I made settlement recommendations, I needed convincing both that the Shalanites were actually *bad guys* and also irrelevant.

A quavering voice cut through the looping message—*I annex this bank*—to answer Rzis's demands. "I am on Shalanite property here. We are not pursuant to the changing whims of the PRE."

Rzis growled. "The Protectors' Office does not agree

and will be required to use force if you do not stand down," he responded. "Please desist in this action and release your hostages."

A sharp, high laugh. Like I said, no one ever changes his mind at this point. That moment was long gone. "Hostages? These are newly made citizens of the Shalanite Supremacy."

"As citizens," Rzis's loud voice rumbled over the wind, unaugmented by any sort of horn or loudspeaker, "they should be able to leave. Elsajh recognizes their travel as foreign citizens."

More laughter from the inside. I guess that meant those new citizens hadn't had passports made yet. As far as I'd seen, the worst offense the Shalanite had committed was monopolizing all the teller machines. No big deal, y'know? Unless those *new citizens* were going to be killed off for sneezing out of turn or something.

Rzis's linen shirt clung to his scapula, dampness twinning it and his muscled back. I figured the profuse sweating equated to *hostages in danger*.

Well, if Rzis could only keep the guy busy, at least I could be productive. There were no rules about my involvement. I mean, technically I wasn't here. I wasn't Zean. I'd never shown a passport or given my name. The real Zean was on walkabout, and I was a non-entity. A non-entity who really hated it when people killed other unsuspecting people. Maybe it's a Terran thing. Maybe it's a Maya Qaitra thing. Either hypothesis you like, I was getting those hostages—new Shalanites, whatever—out of there.

I returned to my hiding place in order to switch back into my leonine form. Quiet as you please, I padded around the building till I found a door to jimmy with a strong claw. A *snick*, a jiggle, and voilà! Terran cat walking. I slunk down empty corridors till I heard the Shalanite's voice.

He was going on about vaporizing any citizen who defected to the occupiers—this being a bank annexed under martial law—and "everybody better stay planted where they are or else." He held up some sort of stick weapon thing, presumably the vaporizer, that whined and whirred so sharply I raised a paw to cover one of my delicate ears.

No time for dramatics, Maya. If he really could reduce a hostage to component atoms, given the correct motivation, I had to ensure he lost the chance.

Rzis called out to him again, more distressed in the wake of that whirring, and distracted the Shalanite from his hostages. I butted my head against the elbow of the closest captive, trying my best to act like a tamed, unthreatening kitty-cat. This was the trickiest part. So long as the hostages kept their cool about the huge, sentient predator in their midst, I should be able to get 'em out my jimmied door. If they panicked and drew his attention or refused to escape with *me*, this'd go up in flames with no oxygen reserves. And like flames, that'd end with dead hostages. Probably a dead or injured Maya, too.

The head-butt victim took it without flinching. He even leaned into me. Huh. That suggested positive race relations for Baastet's Children across all Elsajh's social classes, unless he was just under stress, or was the weird hostage out. The hostages had been roped together rather inexpertly. Further down the line, a few tried to untie themselves. I took the Alexandrian approach. A quick slash of the claw and no more rope.

Down the line I went, freeing *citizens* and herding them into the hallway. The final hostage was giving me a scritch behind the ears when the Shalanite took stock of his situation: completely out of his control.

"Get back here!" he yelled, waving his whirring stick thing at the crowd.

Yeah, buddy. Like that's gonna happen. In fact, his posturing touched off a stampede of hostages out the door I'd used to enter. I made sure they were all getting good and gone, and let the guy take whining potshots at me, twisting to evade the merest touch of energy or bullet—whatever it was they used as weaponry on this planet,; Rzis would know—as I progressed toward the front door to keep him away from the escapees.

Rzis's voice rose louder and louder outside, but I was too busy to distinguish the words. He was probably worried about hostages being killed.

While the Shalanite's weapon was charging back up between uses, I used my tail to swat the stick-thing weapon from his hand. Then I pounced on him, and we rolled out the front door to land, panting, before Rzis. I kept the guy pinned beneath my weight, paws on his shoulders with claws unsheathed, and gave Zean's intended an innocent meow.

"Hold! Hold!" Rzis shouted frantically to the guys behind him, also outfitted in those silly linen pants. They must've been backup from the Protectors' Office. Wonder when they got here. He waited until his buddies had my captive in chains before he reached forward and pulled on my ears. *Ow!* "What were you thinking?" Aww. How sweet. He did care. Okay, that wasn't fair. Rzis was a genuinely nice guy and clearly fond of his bride-to-be, whom I was impersonating. Sorta.

"Those guys are crazy, and you know it!" He growled in frustration. "You could have died." He pulled my ears again, but not as harshly. "You could have died." He turned his back, and I couldn't let it go at that.

I nudged my nose against his hand, smelling his salty anxiety and the spicy heat in his blood.

"No," he said, though he ran his palm over my head. "I've got to make my report. We'll have to talk about this later. That's *talk*. You know," he classified sarcastically, "that thing you do with a mouth and voice box. It does not include running and mriaowing."

I almost changed then. He deserved the respect. We'd been through action together, and he really did seem worried about me. But it wouldn't do any good, and there were so many witnesses. Any of whom might know what Zean looked like hominid. So I nudged his hand again in acknowledgement and loped back down the dusty roads to Zean's house. Alone.

# Chapter Six

*I swear, Mum! It was all Zean's fault.*
*– Zean's brothers, all the time*

**TESTIMONY ENTERED INTO RECORD.**

**From the deposition of Zean Skyline (alien, Elsajh native).**

**Courtesy of the Elsajh Protectors' Office.**

After she'd spent a few days as a kitten, prancing in the sodium lights and pretending she hadn't a care in the world, Zean booked passage for *home*. Surely her parents' Chosen had given up on marrying her by now!

Besides, the station was terribly dull and she missed her lover. She always missed Szueckr when she was away.

Worse, left to his own devices, Szueckr tended to accidentally starve himself. This had led to a fainting spells during street shows. He did so much better when she was there to make sure he had both money and inclination equal to his needs. She decided her first order of action on planet would be to check in on her absentminded love.

Zean headed for the Sunlight Café. She looked forward to the midday quiet, more than prepared to play a short game of sticks and ask after her lover. Alas, this was not to be. When she arrived, the place swam with patrons, and she opened the inner door onto music and dancing and breaking glass. From the looks of things, the party had been going on for days.

Larra, one of Zean's best burlesque dancers, stumbled into her. The diva bounced off and frowned. "I'm not talking to you!" Larra declared.

Zean took a breath, intending to soothe her tangled feelings. She'd apologize for the imagined offense. Melodramatic dancers purred with satisfaction when you pretended they were correct about everything.

Before she could speak, a cheer shook the glass walls. Anonymous hands pulled her into the party, passed her from hug to handshake to cheek-meet.

Thankfully, the strange game of Thread the Zean ended, and she sat heavily at the counter, next to a glum-looking Szueckr. She nudged him to acquire his attention. Surely he wouldn't ignore her once he knew she was there.

"Hey, baby." She brushed their cheeks together

lightly, expecting him to increase the contact and the pressure. "I missed you."

He gave her a sullen look. "I'm sure you did." Then he turned away.

Zean was still trying to figure out how to respond to that when he whipped back around, incensed and so different from the relaxed lover she'd left mere days before. "At least you could have told me! You know that I'd support you in anything you wanted. I could've patched you up if you got hurt. And then we didn't hear from you." He reached out to stroke her cheek before snatching his hand back. "Sure you can take care of yourself, but what about the people who love you, hmm? We're not important anymore? You'd rather cavort with the other Skylines in the Protectors' Office? Finished slumming, did you?"

"What?" She thought they'd got past his insecurities years ago. Yes, she was Skyline. No, she didn't intend to live in that rarefied society. She wanted to stay here with her friends and live with her love. To ply a trade, even.

"Don't you 'what' me!" He picked up his glass only to slam it on the bar. It cracked. "This isn't some little 'family thing' you can sweep aside with your Sky Cursed tail. I had to write music for an interpretive dance of the whole incident. All without knowing whether you were all right." He smoothed slender fingers over the cracks he'd just created.

"An interpretive dance?" She injected the right amount of disbelief to imply that she found the dance quizzical, rather than that she had no idea what *the whole incident* might mean.

"I don't really like the lyrics, though," he said, apparently forgetting his anger in the desire to share. He never liked his lyrics.

"I'm sure they're fine."

Szueckr took this as encouragement to recite some for her, providing Zean a few details of the curious happenings in her absence.

She leaned in, the better to hear in this crush of noisy partygoers.

> Zean's gone 'round the back
> With Skyline's gallantry.
> Zean's come out the front,
> Distracting the fanatic-ry.
> Zean will free
> Elsajh's people readily!
> She stands for the PRE—
> She's the hero of Margavi!

"What do you think?"

"Margavi the bank?" She asked, incredulous. "Also, 'fanatic-ry'?"

"Well, obviously the bank. And you try coming up with a rhyme better than 'fanatic-ry'," he accused. "Especially if you don't want to mention the Shala-nites by name. They don't deserve any publicity, bad or otherwise."

"Baby," she picked her words carefully, "I need you to put aside your doubts for a moment."

The lines around his mouth softened. Szueckr always knew when to treat her seriously. She'd never give him up, and certainly not for whomever her parents had wanted her to meet.

"I think I'm going crazy," she said. "Or maybe the rest of you are. Or, no. No. It's me."

Szueckr took her hand in his furless one and led her away from the party. They sat on the store room steps, quiet. "What's wrong, lovely?"

Oh, how good to hear that pet name from his lips again! "I have no clue what you're talking about."

He smacked her hand. "Inside," he almost whined. His brows furrowed, and his nose took in a long sniff that narrowed its sides. "You said you were going crazy."

"Exactly," she replied. "I must be going crazy because I don't know what anyone's talking about. Why are you writing songs about me? Why is there a party? Why were you so upset with me earlier? As far as I know, I left you with a kiss and a grocer's delivery three days ago."

He dropped her hand and stood up. "I don't believe you just said that to me."

"I really, truly have no idea."

He pressed his lips together, hard enough to turn them yellow. "If you left three days ago, when did you get back?"

"Are you kidding? The first thing I did was come for you. My parents can wait a little longer." She hated the look on his face. It accused her of lying and hurting his feelings on purpose. "Please, can't you at least pretend I'm telling the truth? I deserve that much."

"Pretend. Pretend?" When a lyricist stooped to repetition, it meant he was too incensed to think clearly. "Shall I *pretend* you didn't run off with the Skyline your parents chose for you? Shall we *pretend* you didn't rescue thirty-two hostages when Margavi bank got annexed by a Shalanite? Should everyone in there"—he cocked his head in the direction the party—"*pretend* to forget how you slipped in, freed them all, and then attacked the Shalanite with nothing but naked claws? I think the news called it *a return to the myths of the Sky People.*"

"I swear to you! As far as I know, I've been away these last three days." She had no idea what he was talking about, but for now she needed to save her relationship more than she needed to understand goings-on. She scrambled to her knees before him. "Please, believe me."

His low voice was a scream in the quiet storage area. "How can I? This was your chance to tell me the truth or make up some brilliant excuse, and you wasted it."

Her fingers went cold. "Can you forgive me?" That was the true question.

"No. I *saw* you at that bank with my own eyes." He ran a hand through her hair, not fondness but goodbye. "We're over."

He left her on her knees on the storage steps. Alone for the first time in four years.

# Chapter Seven

*Burlesque may be an art form, but it's not a*
*respectable one.*
*– Anonymous*

**You know, you probably could have avoided
some of the drama surrounding your actions at
the bank by coming clean sooner.**

Gee, ma'am, I never thought of that. And, afterward, of
course I didn't explain to *anyone* about my true nature.

**Sarcasm doesn't work well in transcripts, Qaitra.
So why the Hell didn't you at least explain your
situation to that Protector boyfriend of yours?**

You told me not to, ma'am.

**What? I did?**

Once I was on positive terms with the local powers

that be, if entirely by accident, you seemed to think I'd be of more use to the cause while in disguise.

>**Now you're just trying to get me in trouble on the record, Mahdan.**

Is it working?

>**Like you, I have discretion in the field.**

All the dust was taking permanent residence in my fur. You know how we call most planets *dirtball*? This one was a *dust*ball. I despaired of ever washing it out, and it tasted terrible on my sandy tongue. I'd checked. Multiple times.

I trotted past lilac weeds and rubbed against velvety trees, rehearsing what I would say to Zean's family when I arrived at their house. Planning wasn't my forte, but, well... I wanted to tell them about the identity switch. I'd learned enough to know that these were a civilized people. Besides, this could end horribly for me if they found out on their own. It'd be *Off with her head!* or maybe *Declaw the liar!*

Moreover, her parents deserved to know their daughter was missing. Since I was here, nobody knew to look for a missing person... Oh God. I hadn't thought of that before. This kid was probably in danger because I'd been too happy to assume her identity and go sightseeing at her corner store.

Right, so I wanted to come clean. Maybe they'd help me figure out whom to approach for the first contact spiel—*"We are an exploration and scientific mission from the planet Earth"*—or maybe they'd kick me out and have me arrested. But I wanted out before I muddled any deeper. I'd finished my initial observations, now I would tell the truth.

And Rzis. He deserved to have a first date with his *true* intended. He hadn't signed up for some bizarre E-Tee impostor's crashing his party. Even if he and I got on like fire and oxygen. No, something less destructive than that. We got on like things that couple really well together. Oooh! Tuna and catnip.

Anyway, he ought to meet the woman he planned to marry before, say, the wedding. I was only a copy, standing between him and the woman who possibly got kidnapped.

I arrived home to an obnoxious brother making comments about my *true love* and saying that our mother wanted us to pick up the stuff on a shopping list. Why couldn't *he* take the fluffin' shopping trip?

I decided he was mentally incapable.

"And Little Zee-zee's got a job." The obnoxious brother sounded more proud than mocking, but I swiped a paw at him anyway. On principle. He tumbled back like a kitten might. "Mum volunteered you because it's all your fault we're having a big political summit meeting."

Apparently, there was a summit thanks to "Zean" and her exploits, little brother explained to me. Well, it was more that some high-up VIPs decided the Shalanite threat needed to be countered in a more organized manner in the wake of the bank thing. My adventures were merely an excuse. Anyway, the whole family was on the entertainment committee. How this meant that I—as Zean—ended up as the entertainment coordinator, I had no idea. Well, other than that Zean's mother had volunteered me. Us. Zean. I'd never planned so much as a Terran birthday party, much less a political summit thing.

Zean's brother shoved the shopping list at me, and I snapped it between my teeth, a little too close to the fingers for his comfort. Then I loped off between the wildflowers toward the tree line to find a secluded spot. I looked right, looked left, and scrabbled up into the amethyst pines, claws sinking into the lusciously soft bark.

My tail lashed from side to side, just to keep my balance, and then I shifted to hominid. I had a report to make, a duty to my own people before my duty to *these* people. "Hey there, commander ma'am," I whispered into my *For the millionth time, we don't call them telephones anymore.* If the ship was close enough to the planet, we'd be able to have a realtime conversation.

I listened to the static for *ages*, at least two minutes, before giving up and tapping a quick note about the big political hafla coming up. I included that I—well, my alter ego, sorta—was the guest of honor-ish.

In moments I got a reply, so the ship must have been close enough for data transfer but not for chatting. Or the commander was in the bathroom, or getting drunk, or starting a station-wide brawl, or learning to speak one of the languages that's all growls and clicks. I bit my nail to keep my smile tiny.

Anyway, the tele from my commander said he'd be on Elsajh—correct spelling, apparently—in a couple of days and that I was to maintain my cover identity until I had backup on scene. We'd use the summit as an opportunity to give our spiel in front of all the noteworthies at once.

I whined in the back of my throat, the sound reverberating up through my nasal passages. Keep my cover? But what about Zean? She could be dead or hurting, and her parents wouldn't be happy to find out at the summit thingie. I typed out another message saying as much, and the quick reply was: *Fine. Tell the parents if you trust their discretion. But that's it. Now scamper off to work, Mahdan.*

Sheesh. Everyone always wants me to work. They say, "Maya, polish the zero-g harnesses that you coated with peanut butter last week." Or "Maya, find a species we can mingle genes with." Or "Maya, organize the entertainment for some major E-Tee VIPs."

Okay, that last one was intended more for Zean than for Maya, but I still got stuck with the work. Hey, once I divulged my identity, I could gracefully bow out of planning a huge event.

I bounded across the tall, periwinkle grass, leaping over imagined obstacles and dodging shadowy kitten-catchers, like I used to do as a cub. The stone walls of the family home loomed ahead of me. Three choices: slow down, run into them, or run *up*. I pounced on the building. One claw sank into mortar, and the rest scratch-scrabbled on the rock. Hind legs swinging freely, I heaved upward until I achieved a window ledge on the second floor.

Hah! Totally the window ledge I was going for. I should mark up a new pin for my uniform. *Best Pouncer Ever.*

Zean's oldest brother opened said window next to me, and I almost fell off the building into the waiting wildflowers below. He yanked me inside by the scruff, and I spared a moment to be grateful I hadn't fallen down and lost my eyes in a waiting briar patch or something. Not that they had a briar patch.

"What're you doing in Da's office?" he asked.

I whined and pressed my belly to the ground, scratched at the floor.

"Are we really playing charades?"

I tilted my head at him. I love the *clueless kitten* game. Especially the part where it *really* annoys the guys on second watch. Simpson likes to egg me on whenever he sees me tormenting them with it.

"If you won't talk to me, will you talk to Da?"

*Yes!* I surged forward and nuzzled into his hip, pushing him backward slightly till he tangled fingers in my ruff. I purred for him because I'm nice like that.

He laughed and stroked my ears. That was totally appropriate for *siblings*. "Well, he's not home, but I'll leave him a message for you." He spoke as he wrote so that I could approve it. *"Must talk. Very important. Call me.–Zean."*

I nudged him again to declare the message acceptable because I couldn't very well tell him that calling Zean would be a useless endeavor. Then I leapt out the window, his spluttering disbelief coloring the road sunshine yellow.

That behind me, I had errands to run for the family downtown. Presumably on credit. I wasn't going to let them down. They hadn't asked for an impostor daughter to infringe on their living arrangements. Partway down the dirt road, I found an empty stretch and shifted hominid. Mmmm. I shook out my shoulders and bent my knees in this form's correct direction.

At least I could go out safely and anonymously in my hominid form. Which isn't to say I blended with the crowd. Terran casual attire wasn't remotely in-fashion here.

Where the locals had loose linen pants, I had tight synthetic cotton ones with numerous external pockets. Where they had puffy sleeved jackets that could conceal their hands, I had an open-necked wrap top and an obvious weapon attached to my hip and shoulder. Anything that could make me immediately dangerous was on display.

Plus, no one else was wearing sunglasses. They were essential for hiding my slitted pupils from more excitable passersby.

I strolled along the road, green-tinged sunshine dappled by nine-pointed leaves from all the trees. They liked trees on this planet. I'd link up with Zean's parents and explain the situation when I got back with the stuff on the shopping list. Which I couldn't read and would have to give to a shop attendant. Hopefully without wandering into completely the wrong shop when doing so.

And hopefully without running into Rzis. I'd been avoiding him. He was such a great guy—smart, flexible, responsible, clearly worried about me during the confrontation with the Shalanite. He didn't deserve to be lied to anymore.

Now, you'd think when a planet's interstellar tourist season ended, someone like me might raise a bit of notice. Sure, the planet had some non-local visitors, and plenty of interstellar news outlets, but I didn't see a lot of other E-Tee fashion on the street. Still, the locals kept on doing what they would've been doing, as opposed to when I went out in my leonine form and was an immediate celebrity.

I padded past the bank where we'd run into trouble a few days back without anyone paying me any attention at all. Good.

A block away from it, a street dance troupe performed for a decent crowd, maybe fifteen people clapping and laughing along. I squirmed to the front. Aiyah. They were re-enacting my scene with the hostages. This was doomed to follow me everywhere!

Half to avoid the subject matter of the dance and half to learn about this new planet, I asked an audience member, "So, I keep hearing talk about the Sky People. Who are they, exactly?"

The person I'd tried to chat up ignored me, clapping along with the music.

The dancers were very athletic, leaning away in long planks from the "Shalanite" madman, played by a guy whose limbs flew every which direction at nearly impossible angles. How he managed not to hurt himself, I couldn't tell you. They even had a shifter with a blond leonine form to play "Zean" in the dance. She pranced and postured and heroically took down the madman, then paused for applause from the crowd, rolling her shoulders to make her oiled coat shine more in the afternoon light. The audience loved it.

I tried again with another audience member who looked a little bored. "You seen this before?"

The guy shook his head, and I had no idea if that meant *yes* or *no*. Ah, cross-cultural cues. "It's rare to see this troupe edging into gentrified territory."

Yeah, I could've asked what counted as *gentrified* on this planet, but the answer was irrelevant. The prior question had created rapport between us, so now I could ask him about the Sky People. He explained that they'd come to Elsajh a long time ago, a race of advanced beings who could transform themselves into cats. No one was sure what had happened to make them pull up stakes, but their legacy was peace; and their progeny—the Skylines—made sure to keep it, for considerable generations.

The pacification of an entire species sounded creepy. No wonder the Shalanites were so mad. But that was *ages* ago, and I liked the idea: millennia of peaceful coexistence. Heck, even after the destruction of our planet, we needed luck and incentives to keep the remaining Terrans from fighting each other.

A tall musician joined the dancers at the show's end to accept accolades along with the dancers, and the crowd dispersed. Except for me. I wanted to talk to the blond shifter who appeared to be in charge of packing up. If she led the troupe, then she could commit them to performing for the diplo thingie that I was supposed to be coordinating.

So long as they skipped that "Zean, hero of Margavi" piece.

# Chapter Eight

*"I don't want to talk with you."*
*– Szueckr, too many times in the past day*

**TESTIMONY ENTERED INTO RECORD.**

**From the deposition of Zean Skyline (alien, Elsajh native).**

**Courtesy of the Elsajh Protectors' Office.**

Zean snuck out of her parents' house in the early morning chartreuse. She'd slept in the kitchens, cub-sized and miserable to be away from Szueckr's flat. This location had let her overhear her brothers teasing some guy in the night about how Zean needed to be *stalked* instead of courted.

That had to have been her parents' Chosen.

But he'd laughed them off and tossed Horsza on his

back with a soft paw. Not bad for an uptight conserva-
tive who wanted an arranged marriage. But she still
hoped never to meet him.

Later, she'd heard that same guy mock-growling in
the garden and peeked to see him joined by a greatcat
who purred her pleasure at his presence and offered her
bare throat for a lover's caress. They licked and rubbed
and curled around one another under the light of the
dual moons. Good for that woman, bad for Zean's
parents' plans... if the guy really had been her intended.

She padded down the dusty road from the Hill to
the main thoroughfare, then added mass for a larger
form, a runner's lean-legged stride. Wind forced its way
under her fur. The faster she ran, the colder the air.

Now that she was free of the old homestead, that
temporary domicile until she'd reunited with her
beloved, she had only one goal: get Szueckr back.

She'd given him the night apart to calm down,
staying at her parents' instead of their apartment.
Maybe he'd thought about the things she said. Maybe
he'd *trust* her, like he ought to. In her favor, they'd have
to work together. Some woman wanted to hire the
troupe to perform at an event, and his music matched
her choreographies. As they'd planned. The art
trumped the fight. And while they worked on the art,
he'd remember how good they were. Enforced
togetherness.

She opened the door to their flat. Her lover lay in
the dark shadows beside the window, an empty space
next to him. *Her* space, meant for lazing in the
sunbeams and enjoying the now.

60

His eyes cracked open. "Get out."

Dust danced in the near-green light. "It's my studio too." She hadn't meant to say that.

"You can afford to move out."

She clenched her hands and opened them again, letting the repetitive motion take over. She wasn't going to hiss. Or get angry. Nope. "That's not fair."

"Neither's lying to me and treating me like an instrument that never needs restringing." His mouth contorted into a sneer, so alien on his sensitive face. "Sorry I'm not *exciting* enough for you anymore. Not like your Skyline betrothed."

Augh! They'd been over this. "He's not my betrothed. I never even met him." They'd been over *all* of this. She chanced approaching. The light glistened on her still-sweating shoulder. "Come on, baby. You know I wouldn't hurt you."

"Liar!"

"I wouldn't. I've never. Why are you acting like this?" She knew the words were wrong the moment they united with the air.

"Why am *I* acting like this?" He grabbed the closest thing at hand, an earpiece for a long-lost telecomm, and threw it at her. "Get out! I don't want to talk with you. Maybe ever."

She backed toward the door. This had all gone so horribly wrong. "We'll need to talk about the performance for the thing."

"Ever!" he repeated.

She kept backing away till she was out the door. She'd try him again later.

Her own earpiece vibrated against her skull. Ugh. She was so not in the mood. "What?" she snapped.

"Morning, sweetie," her Da said, and she heaved a silent sigh. She'd rather hack a hairball, but he was her Da, so... "I'm sorry I missed you last night. So, what did you want to talk with me about?"

She hadn't been aware anyone had seen her at home. Apparently she'd been left alone thanks to good luck, rather than design. "I don't know what you're talking about." She said that a lot these days.

He laughed as though she'd said something funny. "Well, at least you like that polite young man. I'm so glad the two of you hit it off. Your Mum and I were sure you'd be the perfect match, but she thought you might be too stubborn..."

Stubborn? She was *not* stubborn. But she also wasn't interested in some guy she'd never met. No matter what Szueckr—and apparently Da—thought. "Ugh. Da! I'm not into your new *arranged marriage* project. I'm with my lover right now." Well, he was in the other room, and mad at her, but it counted. "I don't need some near stranger when I have someone already."

The line crackled. "What's that, sweetie?"

"You know I have a lover, Da. We've been together four whole years."

Her Da shouted over her, "What's that? You need me to *crackle* send your lover? I thought he was just your betrothed!" Of course, the telecomms chose this moment to hiss. Just to make this whole conversation with Da awkward. "I'm going to give that youngster a stern talking-to about pre-marital boundaries."

Super awkward. Also, it was so wrong because (a) she hadn't even met her parents' Chosen, and (b) she could totally make her own choices. They'd never complained about her relationship with Szueckr before, so what did the new guy matter? Augh.

"Yeah, Da. You're breaking up."

"Don't you worry, sweetie. I'll send him down to you. Oh, I hope you can hear me."

Looked like she'd be meeting this guy after all. If she could recognize him. Well, he'd stand out if he came down to the Sunlight Café, which was where she needed to be for her appointment with the paying patron. Maybe her luck'd double and he'd refuse to come to her side of town.

# Chapter Nine

*If you must fight, only fight with other Skylines. You*
*have an unfair advantage*
*over those not descended from the Sky People.*
*– Every school principal to every Skyline*
*child ever sent down for fighting*


**TESTIMONY ENTERED INTO RECORD.**

**From the deposition of Rzis Skyline (alien, Elsajh native).**

**Courtesy of the Elsajh Protectors' Office.**


After a thoroughly befuddling talk with Zean's father, Rzis knew one thing for sure: he was supposed to meet her on the less affluent side of town at a place called the Sunlight Café in order to discuss... something of extreme importance.

Her father had started with *glad you and Zean are getting along*. But that had mixed with *I'm not sure she's ready to have sex, possibly ever, and especially with someone she's only known a few days*. Which sounded like disapproval of their budding friendship, if taken to an extreme because Rzis knew he hadn't had sex of any kind with his potential betrothed. Though, Zean's father acknowledged their intended status as a mitigating factor.

In the end, Rzis wasn't sure if her father even wanted the betrothal anymore. And Rzis had done nothing to deserve this scrutiny. Nothing! He'd barely seen the young woman since their run-in with the Shalanite, except for some clandestine nighttime cuddling. Which sounded far more illicit than it actually was. In fact, he'd only been at her parents' residence—and, thus, available for this chewing out—in hopes of fitting their schedules together.

He leapt over a broken slab in the road, the path growing rockier and dustier the closer he got to this Sunlight Café. With her need to save others and her playfulness, Zean might be his ideal intended. Although her summoning him to assignations in strange places and teasing her father with innuendos... well, she was young yet. She'd grow out of that.

He pushed through the spiny undergrowth that took over the road in this less well-kept part of town. A large glass dome grew out of the dusty landscape, one side nearly hidden by a copse of trees, themselves an unexpected spot of violet against the pale plains.

He went through the first door, then the second, both made of glass. It was an interesting effect. In the buffer zone, he realized how quiet a room made of glass could be, after the noise of the road. Then he moved into the real café. Even at midday, the place bustled with gambling and drinking. Chairs scraped across the wooden floor. Spoons clinked inside of soup bowls.

Since Zean neither bounded over nor waved arms while screaming his name, Rzis cast about for an official person whom he could ask for her whereabouts. Most of the clientele sat in groups of two or more, a category he'd join when he found his erstwhile companion. One singleton occupied a wooden table, but he definitely wasn't the official type. He was slumped over the worn-smooth planking, shoulders hunched and one hand supporting his head while the other held a glass of something so heavily fermented Rzis could have smelled it even without the Skyline nose. An oily puddle on the tabletop reflected the man's pale gold eyes, then dripped into an expanding slick on the floor.

No, not an official type at all.

Rzis cleared his throat, hoping to get the attention of some unseen shop owner. Only the despondent drunkard looked up—

And growled, a passable rendition of a greatcat from a non-Skyline throat. "You!"

Rzis checked behind him. Having never encountered this person before, he was fairly sure there was no *done him wrong* story in their nonexistent shared past.

A few spoons clinked their last, then quieted. All focus on the brewing discord. About which Rzis knew nothing.

The man lurched up, his table creaking and skittering backwards. "You! I won't stand for it. You won't get away with this." Surely some friend should be helping the belligerent fool to sit back down at his table.

Rzis took a smooth step away, maintaining the space between them. He had no interest in fighting a weakling over some imagined slight.

A heckler called, "You tell him, buddy!"

"Hah!" The man waved his hand, then swayed to compensate. "She's *my* love. I love her more." He barreled forward and caught Rzis about the waist in a childish approximation of a grappler's unbreakable hold. "I was here first!"

Rzis gently removed the invading arms from his person. "I'm not sure who you mean. Why don't we sit down and discuss—"

"Zean! Your *intended.*" The man said it like a curse. "Well, I won't give her up without a fight. After all, she doesn't even remember going off with you." He jabbed toward Rzis's chest and missed. Grumbled, "Privileged Skylines."

Rzis held out his hands, placating, even as he swallowed a cub-sized ball of bile. He wouldn't let the disappointment show on his face. "You're quite correct. If she'd rather be with you, then I won't stand in the way." Though he'd have appreciated being *told* rather than shoved into unknowing confrontation with his supposed rival. "I'm beginning to think she's too impetuous for me, after all."

The drunk straightened, creakily slow, and wound back his arm in the most obvious *about to punch you* motion Rzis had ever witnessed.

Rzis side-stepped out of the way.

"She's too good for both of us! Too good for anyone. But I'm a-gonna fight for her." He threw another easily avoided punch. "She doesn't even 'member you, 'member Margavi. Says she was off-planet."

Again, Rzis dodged a forward rush, using a guiding hand at the end to direct his counterpart into a chair. "You said that already."

"Off-planet. Don' care if it's a lie." The man lolled back, his shoulders going over the chair and his dark hair brushing the table behind him. "I c'n forgive her and we can live together and move on and be my love. She can call a doctor for the mem'ry stuff if she wants."

"That sounds like the perfect plan." Rzis patted him on the shoulder, soothing. *She should have told me herself.* These two deserved each other.

He surged out of the chair. "You!" Again.

Rzis heaved a sigh and danced backward at Skyline speeds.

This didn't stop his assailant, who powered forward, determined to catch and damage his rival. With the speed involved, Rzis would have hurt the man if he dodged or deflected, and that wouldn't be fair to the addled, lovesick swain. Instead, Rzis opened his arms so his attacker would bury momentum in forgiving muscle.

But the rusher slipped backward on the floor—on nothing?—and slid heels-first between Rzis's braced legs. *Thunk.* He hit his head on the way down.

Dropping to his knees, Rzis checked the man's vitals. To the whole café, he announced, "He'll be zooming about in no time. Only a small bump mixed with the liquor."

Nothing happened in the wake of this announcement. The place remained silent. No glasses moved. No odds-and-evens sticks rattled or clattered to a playing surface.

"I don't suppose any of you have seen Zean?"

A cough.

Rzis flowed to his feet. He knew when he wasn't welcome. He brushed the detritus from his knees. The floor stuck to his legs even after he'd stalked out the café's door.

As a thought experiment, Rzis chose to assume, for a moment, that the drunk talked sense and Zean's memory was suspect. Assumed also that she was not afflicted by some strange schizophrenia, for he'd seen no signs of it. In that case, the Zean whom Rzis knew could only be a pretender!

But what could one Skyline gain from fooling another? The community was small enough that the ruse would be nearly impossible to maintain. Besides, no two Skylines had identical two-legged forms. Then again, he had never seen Zean's two-legged form, only her Sky Person one.

The true Sky People, the ones who had uplifted the population of Elsajh, had been masters of the four-footed body, eschewing all others. If they had returned at long last to see what great works their descendants had crafted, of course they'd observe before revealing themselves.

*Stars preserve me!* Rzis had flirted with one of *the Sky People.*

Perhaps, if he proved himself to her, she would reveal her plans for his world.

# Chapter Ten

*Keep a hold of your tail. You don't want to end up like*
*a lynx, do you?*
*–Terran cubs' taunt*

**So, when *did* you tell your Protector buddy about being an alien from the planet Earth? I know it was sometime before the big shootout.**

What makes you think he didn't figure it out himself? He's a smart cookie, and it's his job to ferret out secrets like this one.

**No one expects an alien to masquerade as his fiancée.**

Are you sure you're allowed to interrupt like this when I'm on the record? Just let me tell the story in order. Ma'am.

The dance troupe feline had asked me to meet her at the Sunlight Café to settle on the performance details. It was in an area I hadn't seen yet, being familiar mostly with downtown and Zean's parents' residence. Clearly, I was missing out! Shoppers bustled in the chartreuse streets. Others called out for me to *experience local culture* with delicacies from their food carts. I was pretty sure I saw some sort of covert, polyhedral dice game.

The Sunlight Café reminded me of the old biodome experiments. Largely because it was a dome. Only one story, but lofted to get as much natural light as possible. The whole thing was made of windows. Oh! They'd constructed a dome within a dome to keep the elements out but the sunlight in. Neat.

A patron exited, his broad shoulders slumped. Powerful thighs propelled him through the doors, and I took a brief moment to appreciate the play of warm muscle on a dusky man.

Then I recognized him. Rzis. Fluffy damnation. I wasn't ready to see him yet. I'd barely managed to keep my peace last night while we flirted and piled together in a snug ball of contentment and desire. Directing our budding relationship along platonic lines grew more difficult with every passing cuddly caress. Partially because of developing expectations and partially because I wanted to spend time with him as me. I couldn't keep putting him off with leonine-only activities much longer.

Truth be told, I didn't want to. I wanted him to know *Maya*, even if we only did the same things as when I was

Zean. We played, we fought, we planned, we plotted. We licked, we touched, we slept. But to do those things as a hominid woman! To speak my thoughts, to hear his life, to press fingertips to resilient skin...

But I still had to tell Zean's parents about my identity before I could even consider telling him. There was nothing for it. I had to hide.

I transformed and leapt up through the branches of the nearest tree. I couldn't be found. Fantasies aside, he wasn't likely to declare his everlasting love and devotion to the Terran he'd unwittingly hooked up with. No, I'd have to play *hide and please don't seek* until my shipmates arrived. Being outed as an identity thief, before I had backup on hand, would just be bad. Assuming he figured it out. Assuming I told him.

Hey, what was he doing so far from the Skyline side of town anyway?

I growled low in my throat and settled my chin on my paws. This whole situation was a mess, and I was looking forward to its being over. So long as *over* didn't mean *Maya Qaitra strung up by her neck and choked to death*. That wouldn't be fun.

I flicked my tail in annoyance. Or I tried to. Thing wouldn't budge. Either I'd received spinal damage from nowhere, or I'd fallen prey to the oldest cliché ever: cat stuck in a tree. If I *had* to get stuck in the tree, did it have to be by my tail?

Sighing quietly—I was still trying to hide from Rzis, after all—I flipped around to see what my tail had managed to get itself into. I swear, the thing's got a mind of its own sometimes.

73

This was not one of those times. My tail hadn't wormed its way between tree branches nor made friends with some kind of heavy-duty E-Tee sap. Nope. It was pinned by the shiny, black paw of the very feline I was avoiding. How did he get up here without my hearing it? Sneaking up on a fully trained Mahdan is no easy matter.

I tried to look innocent and blinked slowly in that brainless kit style. "Mew?"

He slid into his hominid form and smirked at me. "The tail gave you away," he said. "Can we talk?"

I knew when I was caught. Anchoring myself to the tree branch as well as possible, I transformed. I put on my sunglasses before he could notice my slitted eyes and hid my furless face behind a mess of blond hair. No reason to give myself away too soon.

"That's an interesting outfit," Rzis said, too casual to be real. "Is it for something?"

I grinned behind my hair. *You like living dangerously, buddy.* If I'd been the real Zean, I could've taken that as an insult to my tastes. He'd lucked out in getting the wrong woman. I mumbled to disguise my Terran accent, "I'm thinking of starting a new trend." That was a good answer. Provided zero information while still being extremely flirtatious, which kept my cover.

At least, among Terrans it would be considered flirtatious and information-free. I had to remember that I didn't know anything about these people, and didn't have the leeway that came with the *we are peaceful explorers* spiel I usually gave first thing. Anything I thought I knew could be a dead giveaway that I wasn't really from around here. Or anywhere near here. Or this star system.

"Starting a trend?" he repeated.

Sounded like he needed a bit more experience with women and the ways they worked to shape society. Throughout history, it has been a feminine prerogative to gain power via fashion, among other outlets. *For Terrans.* "Never mind."

"So," he started a new topic. "It was really impressive how you helped us out with that Shavardian conflict the other day."

Right. Of course he'd want to talk about that thing at the bank. I thought the guy had been called a *Shalanite*? I could've been wrong, and besides, I had to go with the flow. "It was no big deal." I tried for modesty. Please let that be enough. That situation had *political minefield* written all over it, and I knew absolutely nothing about the cultural context.

"I've never seen a Shavardian tricked that way." He watched me with intense, dark eyes, as though he could penetrate this curtain of messy hair which I'd so carefully placed between us.

Couldn't he drop it? Starting fashion trends seemed a lot less sticky. "Well, you know. Couldn't let those Shavardians get the drop on honest citizens." I nodded, letting my body language close the subject. Maybe I could learn something about him now, something just for me, not for the cause. I wanted a tidbit I could hold close to my heart and know was *mine.* "So, what've you been up to since I saw you last?"

He lunged forward and wrapped a hand behind my

nape, where you'd scruff a kitten. The heat of his body soaked into mine, and I wanted to sway forward into him, but his grip kept me still, separate. Fluffy damn. I'd stepped into something, and it wasn't a romantic courtship ritual. "Who are you?" he hissed into my face.

I started to laugh off the accusation, hoping he'd buy it, but he only tightened the hand on my nape and growled at my attempt to get away. I *knew* talking about politics had been a bad idea. How was I going to get out of this? At this point, I couldn't keep up the Zean disguise. The best I could hope for was *benevolent outsider*.

"You're not from around here, that's for sure." He deepened his voice into a bone-vibrating growl. "You aren't Zean."

"Okay, okay!" I pushed up my sunglasses and looked into his eyes, giving him his first look at my slit pupils and enjoying the surprised hiss he couldn't hold in. That's right, pal. You have no idea what you're dealing with, so you'd better stop threatening the mystery woman. "I'm not Zean. I'm just checking out your planet. Nothing major." I tried to twist in his grip. "Would you mind letting go? I won't run off."

His warm, strong fingers released me, and I kneaded my nape, half wishing my hand was his and half grateful that he'd let me go. He leaned closer to watch my pupils expand and contract at his nearness. "Are you one of the Sky People, then?" His breath washed over my mouth in a proto-kiss. He grabbed my hands in his, squeezing gently.

According to the legends I'd heard, these Sky People had abandoned Elsajh millennia ago. Since Baastet's Children had only been engineered two hundred fifty years ago, that was an unqualified *Ha! No.* Also, we didn't believe in pacification and uplift and messing with other people's cultures, only preserving our own.

So I gave him an abbreviated version of the first contact speech. *From Terra, looking to explore the universe and meet new friends, would love to leave a few diplomats and scientists on the planet for cultural study and exchange,* and so forth. As usual, I left out the follow-on bits—raising children on your world, making sure Terra lived on, creating a Little Terra everywhere we went—but those things weren't important to this generation. Not really.

He frowned and slid away from me to lean against the tree trunk. "I'd hoped the Sky People had returned to us. You've been such... been so..." Bravado seeped out of him as he trailed off, his hands trailing off mine as a parallel. The shivery touch made my heartbeat quicken.

"Does it matter?" I didn't want it to matter. I'd hoped that once he knew the truth, he'd stand with me. I mean, clearly, my alienness wasn't the problem. This star system was pretty fluffin' open to aliens. The station I'd been found on was proof enough of that—four inhabited planets in the system with two more next door, and they all hung out together—one more alien group would be *somewhat interesting*, rather than *world-shattering*.

I was beyond thankful for that. I was already in enough trouble here by impersonating a local and having tried to fool this guy from the Protectors' Office. At least having a leonine form united me in good company with these Sky People. If this had been any other world, I'd have been strung up in the public square or downtown or wherever.

He shook his head, backing further into the tree trunk. Further away from me, and I tremored in the sudden cold. "I don't even know who you are."

Of *course* he did. The words sunk claws into my gut. It may have only been a few days, but we had history, he and I. We'd trounced my—Zean's—brothers, emerged victorious over the Shalanite, and been working our way from good acquaintances to good friends who cuddle and might be more. "Rzis..." I extended a hand, wanting that touch back, that connection between us. I let my hand hover, leaking heat and waiting for his permission.

"How can I trust you?" he whispered. "Is everything you've ever said to me a lie?" He laughed then, a harsh, broken sound. "No, of course not," he answered his own question. "After all, you've never *talked* to me."

I pulled my unwelcome appendage back. "I wanted to. But I had to keep my cover identity."

"Yes. You couldn't let anyone know you weren't—" He leaned forward with an investigator's energy. This wasn't Rzis the Beau anymore. This was Rzis the Protectors' Finest. "What have you done with the real Zean Skyline?"

I brushed a wisp hair off my forehead, wishing I were in leonine form and could actively groom it. "The hunting party mistook me for her on the station, and I never corrected the assumption. She could be anywhere."

He slammed an open hand against the tree trunk, shaking us in its branches, and cursed. "I should arrest you for kidnapping and possible murder." But he made no move to restrain me or drag me out of our tree. He drew up his knees and buried his head in them. "But I won't. Sky People help me, but I won't. Not yet. Not till I've thought this through."

He looked up at me then, his eyes pulled tight and shiny. He bit the corner of his lip with a growing fang, as though he had no control over his change anymore. "I need some time," he said. And then he transformed completely, leapt down from our branch, and raced off as though all the cat-haters were chasing behind.

...whoa.

I blew out a long breath that teased the blond strand in front of my face. With a shaky inhale of air tainted with his peppery sweat, I firmed my mouth and my resolve.

Right, so I was supposed to meet that dance troupe leader today to hammer out the details of her performance at the summit meeting. I changed my hands to paws and clambered to the ground. Hopefully she wouldn't charge too much because I had no idea what any of the local money meant. Rzis might have helped me, but asking him for anything was right out.

# Chapter Eleven

*Bad things happen to those who are pushy.*
*— saying on Elsajh*

**TESTIMONY ENTERED INTO RECORD.**

**From the deposition of Zean Skyline (alien, Elsajh native).**

**Courtesy of the Elsajh Protectors' Office.**

Zean came prepared with a list of potential dances to offer the entertainment coordinator. This could be the event that lifted her troupe to prominence.

When she entered, a loose congregation ringed an obscured spot on the Sunlight Café's floor. Probably someone cheating at sticks dropped one. Again. One of the knot noticed her arrival and whispered to the person next to him, who mumbled to the person next to her. And so on. Until everyone stared at Zean, silent. Their gazes sat heavily on her lungs.

"What?"

The floor groaned a response, a familiar sound.

She dashed to the semi-circle of patrons and slid to her knees at Szueckr's side on the planking. "Sky People above! What happened?"

He pushed weakly at her fluttering hands. "What? Your *new* lover didn't tell you?"

Not this again. "I am so confused right now." Well, she'd let him get away with it this time. He was hurt. Still, she bit her lower lip hard enough to make indents while she gathered an abandoned sweater from the back of a chair and tried to bundle it beneath his head.

He rolled out of her quasi-embrace and pushed himself up on shaking arms. "Tell the truth for once." Like she hadn't been telling it this whole time!

He didn't give her the chance to protest her truthiness. He deserted her for a nearby odds-and-evens game. He hobbled to the table and cast the sticks, not waiting for his turn nor placing a bet. The players at the table let him join anyway.

All right then. She stalked to the bar, carefully keeping her back to Szueckr. She wouldn't chase him. Her fur didn't cling to the furniture. She didn't see him. He wasn't there.

"Excuse me?"

Zean angled to the side *not* facing Szueckr. The blond coordinator had joined her, still wearing those oddly dark glasses. "Hello again."

They exchanged pleasantries, and Zean was surprised at the catlike manner in which the blond stretched into the sunbeams. She didn't have any other obvious Skyline characteristics, like the heavier coating of downy fur even in two-legged form, and you didn't see many Skylines down here—Zean herself excepted—much less someone so exalted as an entertainment coordinator. You had to know someone important or *be* someone important to get a job like that.

The coordinator—who rudely hadn't given a name; maybe she didn't want it known that she'd been down to this side of town?—listened to Zean's dance list and frowned. "Would you mind not doing the interpretative re-enactment of Zean's heroic freeing of Shalanite hostages?"

The dance really needed a better name than that. It was far too long. She'd have to work on it. "That's fine. Since I won't be able to dance myself, the troupe doesn't want to do that one anyway." She'd be in attendance as Hero Zean, rather than Dancer Zean. The request was a relief. The troupe had anticipated the coordinator would desire it, the topic being so popular these days.

"Oh, thank goodness." The woman's face opened up with her sudden relaxation, eyes relaxing and mouth showing a pink tongue. *Strange that she's pinkening it. I've never met a Skyline who could do a partial shift before.*

"What have you got against that piece anyway? I mean, you hired us based on seeing it."

The woman blushed. "People will be coming up to me all night as it is. If you do that dance, everyone will be talking about it—and me—for the whole function."

That made absolutely no sense. "Who are you then?"

"I'm Zean, of course."

*What?* Zean looked down at her own body, checking that she hadn't transformed into someone else. Nope, she was still Zean. "You most certainly are not." Besides, they didn't look a thing alike.

The woman—not-Zean—shuffled back from the bar. "Of course I am," she asserted. "It's not like you've met Zean." Then, curiously, "Have you?"

"I know her quite well."

"All right. Let me prove it to you." With that, the blond shifted into a large, dry-grass-colored lion.

The lion looked familiar, and not only because it was one of Zean's own forms.

"You're the woman from the station! What are you doing here, pretending to be me?" More quietly, she added, "And thank you for protecting me from those men."

"From the station?" not-Zean puzzled after shifting back. She took off her dark glasses, revealing disconcertingly animalistic eyes, to peer closer. "You were the *kitten*? You're a lot older than I thought."

Zean laughed, letting herself be distracted. This turn of events was so much better than losing her memory as well as her lover. She'd simply had an altruistic twin, like in the dramas. The woman's two-legged form was obviously not Skyline, being mostly hairless, which meant not-Zean could only be one of the Sky People, returned to Elsajh to do good works and avoiding the fame that came with being a creature of legend. After all, they were the sole other feline shapeshifters in the known universe.

Zean vowed not to make any awkwardness for their benevolent visitor from outside the star system. She'd have to drop the whole subject of the impersonation. "You know what this means?" she crowed.

"Umm, no?"

"It means I can dance at the summit without embarrassing my parents! Do it again." She shaped her hands to represent shifting to a large cat form.

In moments, there were two large cats looking at each other. As if playing a mirror game, they turned to inspect markings and movement. They rubbed along each other's sides, passing back and forth.

Nearby customers adjusted their chairs to watch the spectacle. They didn't usually see more than one Skyline down here, much less identical twins. *But, hey,* she imagined the locals thinking, *While it was strange at the café, who knew what those Skylines got up to?*

Szueckr shuffled over, screwing his foot into the floor. "Zee?" He tentatively reached out to the stranger, patting her head softly, as if she might bite him.

Zean chuffed a laugh and transformed back, quickly followed by her counterpart. Szueckr pulled his arm in, unwinding it from the stranger's hair, and sidled closer to Zean. Tentatively. Good. Let him wonder whether she'd forgive his lack of faith.

Zean put her hands into her sleeves and bowed. "My name is Zean." She said to the other woman, primly as she'd been taught at university. "May all of our meetings be pleasant."

The woman smiled wide and bowed in return, hands on her bare forearms. "My name is Maya. Maya Qaitra. Pleased to meet you."

The café's patrons returned to their normal activities, no longer interested since the dual-Skyline spectacle had ended.

"How do you feel about staying clones a while longer? Because I'd hoped to avoid this formal function. Especially now I know it's all your fault." At Zean's side, Szueckr trembled.

Maya pretended to be put-upon. "That's right, blame it on the Terran."

Szueckr interjected. "Terran? I've never heard of them. Err, you." It was more than an attempt to join her conversation. It was a declaration of intent, intent to be part of her life.

Zean nudged his ankle with her own, tangling their scents together. He pressed in, a warm line of sunshine against her calf.

The Terran, Maya, nodded. "That's probably a good thing. I'm with a team of explorers, very far from our home system. The rest of my team should show up at the summit, actually. We plan to introduce ourselves to all the important dignitaries at once and ask permission to leave a diplomatic and scientific delegation here on Elsajh. I think our people would be a good match." She grinned conspiratorially. "I've been studying you for a few days, you see."

Zean giggled. "And everyone will love you when they find out *you* helped those hostages. 'The Sky People have come again!'" Just like in the children's books.

"So, we're good then?" Maya checked. "I'll be 'Zean' for the family while you dance, and then we'll switch when my commander arrives?"

"Sounds perfect," Zean affirmed. Though she still had one question... "Did you happen to meet my parents' Chosen? I was supposed to be meeting my fiancé-to-be when I left."

Maya bit her lip, but turned the expression into a wobbly smirk. "His name is Rzis. You'll meet him at the summit tomorrow. Don't worry. I didn't marry him for you." She slumped against the bar. "Fair warning: he's very upset with us. Well, with me, really."

Zean recognized that quality of despondent slump. She'd worn it earlier. "We'll find you a better man."

"I liked this one, back when he thought I was you."

Szueckr's arm wrapped around Zean from behind, a belt that secured her to a Szueckr-shaped chair. They were going to be fine. "Then we'll have to show him you're just as good as my favorite cat."

Nuzzling under her lover's chin, Zean basked in the attention from both sides. Love and curiosity. A cat's ambitions fulfilled.

# Chapter Twelve

*We're a peaceful envoy originally from the planet*
*Earth.*
*– Terran first contact script*

**Tell me you're not getting mushy on me, Mahdan.**

Not during a formal inquiry, sir.

**And don't you forget it.**

The day of the summit had come and everything was going smoothly. Outlandishly smoothly. Improbably smoothly. I was expecting disaster at any second.

There had been a few minor instances where Zean was mistaken for herself—how's that for a description?—but these cleared up easily. After all, I was across the room with Zean's family. My leonine form was clearly Zean's—as far as her newfound fame was concerned—so the real Zean had tweaked her own a bit, but not too much. So convenient that the shapeshifters of Elsajh could attain multiple forms, unlike the Terran kind.

For the most part, though, this was a bigwig reception like any other in the universe. I padded along next to Zean's parents. I nodded at people we passed, but was never expected to transform and say anything. As a symbol of what Skylines could achieve, I'd been requested to stay leonine. Handy, since I wasn't ready to show off my alien hominid form.

Let me tell you just how much this would never happen with other Terrans. If one of Baastet's Children was allowed to this kind of Terran event, she'd better be staying hominid. Still, here I was at some big hafla, leonine *and* a guest of honor. My company would be in for a shock when they got here. Oh, you thought I'd warned them? No way on Elsajh. That'd ruin the fun. Here, though, every major notable had a cat shadow. This lot was really into their Sky Person mythology.

Novel as the experience was, however, my tail twitched with anticipation. My company was scheduled to arrive at any moment, and if they could time it so I didn't have to hear any boring speeches about living in harmony or understanding our Shalanite neighbors—well, I'd let the chefs use some of my kibble. Gluttons.

Now, Zean and I had anticipated a few problems that might arise, and I wanted to get to the meat of the event before any of them happened. What kind of problems? Well, someone could point out that Zean and the dancer looked a lot alike. Someone could wonder why anyone of Skyline descent was a common dancer. Zean could change to her two-legged form for a moment and be recognized as herself. And so on.

And Rzis... we knew he'd attend. But was he angry enough to expose us? Or would he just ignore me? I hoped he and I and Zean—thus proving I had nothing to do with her disappearance—could get together at some point in the evening and work out our complicated interrelationships. Every flash of dark hair set my eyes to hopeful shimmering. None of those glimpses were Rzis *yet*, but I knew he'd show eventually.

Anyway, we were coming up on the most delicate part of the switch. Once her dancing was over, but before the real speechifying started—as opposed to this reception—Zean would reclaim her place on the Skyline side of the room and I'd wait in the shadows for my people to join me. After that, the room would have only one Zean in it, meaning no chances of discovery.

This is when Murphy's Law kicked in. I always say that trouble comes looking for me, but I guess Zean and I confused it. I was hiding in an alcove behind the reception room, ready for Zean to come out and switch off.

Waiting. Waiting.

Maybe I should have told my commander about the aliens that transform à la Baastet's Children.

I peeked through the door to check on Zean's progress, still in leonine form, and there was my company, in full dress uniform. A single glance would tell you that we're not from around here. The clothes alone! The Elsajh diplomats wore the dark-colored jackets with high collars and sleeves so big you could hide a kitten in them. Their trousers were stiflingly stiff and so loose they practically counted as circle skirts.

In contrast, my company had gone minimalist. We couldn't hide a fluffy thing. It wouldn't be right. Not in a formal situation, surrounded by important people. The commander was the most formally dressed in skintight white shorts, a pair of straps that crossed to form armor over her heart, and a wristwatch that doubled as a communicator. Her weapons were in plain sight, holstered across her hips. No treachery possible.

I envisioned how things might have gone if she'd started out in the local formalwear. It wouldn't have lasted long:

> *Elsajh native at coat check:* (politely bored) May I take your coat, ma'am?
>
> *Company commander:* Yes, of course. (pause, then desperate with embarrassment) And my jacket, and my shoes, and these pants, and this shirt.
>
> *Coat check:* We only take coats, ma'am.
>
> *Commander:* (desperately, holding up shoes) Please take these feet coats.
>
> *Coat check:* Shall I get a doctor, ma'am?

So my company had made it to the big to-do. And sensibly, they'd gone searching for me, since I know the culture and am the first contact specialist. You don't make contact without your Mahdan unless there are serious circumstances.

But they hadn't found me. They'd found Zean, packing her stuff after finishing the dance performance. My commander was giving her the dressing-down of my career, turning red with splotchy bits of purple. It was *what do you think you're doing?* mixed with *never in my life seen such a disgrace to the Terran condition* followed by *can't you ever be serious?*

Now, admittedly, Zean was basking in the novelty. She hadn't shifted to expose the mistake. Wearing a leonine expression of utmost contentment, she lay on the floor to better soak up the words. If you knew about the mix-up, it was funny. Especially since I was spared the lecture. So long as I didn't end up on the weird rations again.

Unfortunately, not many knew about the mix-up. Just me, Zean, and Rzis. What the locals saw: crazy people attacking their current hero and guest of honor. The large room rumbled with epic agitation.

I heard Rzis saying "She's the dancer!" but no one was listening anymore. This could get messy real fast. My instincts urged flight, but I choked them down. Who needed a Mahdan that ran from trouble? Besides, Rzis was on my side, or at least on the side of *calming things down*. Maybe it wouldn't be so bad. Not if I didn't let it escalate any further.

Leonine again, I dashed through the door and to my commander's side. Zean stood up and rubbed against me in a greeting of close friends. The room fell silent as everyone watched our mirror-like spectacle. I twitched an ear at her, and she swatted it before heading over to her family, still leonine.

I shifted hominid. Time to tell Elsajh that there were new aliens on the block. I saluted my commander, something I never did outside of diplomatic situations. "Mahdan first class, Maya Qaitra, ma'am."

She took it well, the commander. She turned from me and bowed in Zean's direction. "My apologies, ma'am. I mistook you for this scamp here."

Zean matched her, going hominid and bowing with her hands in her sleeves. "My forgiveness," she replied. "It's an easy mistake to make." She grinned widely, and I knew she couldn't hold it in anymore. "After all, she's been fooling everyone I know for days!"

And the noise in the room picked up. As we'd expected it would. My commander gave me a look that said, *We are talking about this later, and I might bust you down to second class, Baastard*. But she couldn't do that now. Now we were going to do the standard meet-and-greet. Sort of a *Hi, we're here. Wouldn't you love to hang out?*

We didn't get the chance. People mobbed us, all ignoring the commander in order to talk to me:

"Were you at Margavi?"

"Are more Sky People returning?"

"Will you stay here or go with these rude men?"

The commander and I shared a significant look. If there was a *request* for Terran presence, that was even better than convincing E-Tees that we should be friends. Unfortunately, I wasn't really one of their mythological Sky People, which might cause a problem.

I held up a hand for silence, but didn't get it. Well, what was the good of being a place you can shift if you don't take the opportunity, right? I shifted to leonine and roared. Loudly.

Silence. Hah!

I shifted back. "To answer your questions. Yes, I was the lion at Margavi. Zean here"—I motioned to my counterpart—"was unavailable." There was a loud, happy rumble and a bit of cheering off to the side. "However," I continued, "I am not one of your Sky People. I've never met any of them. In fact, I used to think my kin were the only ones like us." This was the perfect opening for the first contact script.

"I'm a Terran. We"—here I gestured to the rest of the company—"are an envoy originally from the planet Earth. We would like to open peaceful diplomatic relations with the people of Elsajh."

# Chapter Thirteen

*There's always someone stronger, faster, smarter.*
*Make those people your friends. Enviable friends trump*
*enviable enemies.*
*– From* The Sky People's Wisdom, *third edition*

**TESTIMONY ENTERED INTO RECORD.**

**From the deposition of Rzis Skyline (alien, Elsajh native).**

**Courtesy of the Elsajh Protectors' Office.**

*Peaceful diplomatic relations?* The loud woman, clearly in a position of power over not-Zean, followed up her introduction with speeches that said all the right words. *Share our knowledge with you* and *Understand the values of your culture.* But how could Rzis take the woman at her word when she demonstrated the willingness to enforce those supposedly peaceful desires with the weapon boldly attached to her hip?

This was clearly an advance force for a potentially hostile invasion. They knew the diplomatic lingo, but one couldn't mistake their true message. These *Terrans* appeared on the second floor of a heavily fortified building, having intimidated their way past security on the lower floors, and had the temerity to threaten a room full of Elsajh's most important personages. A silent threat was still a threat, and Rzis recognized the weaponry, worn openly on their bodies for all to witness. Such projectile motion armaments had a prominent place on the Protectors' *banned items* list for non-locals.

The tubes and handgrips stayed safely holstered, but screamed militaristic intent. Rzis had been a fool to trust Zean's impersonator. It was one thing to keep quiet about Skylines switching places with each other, another to shelter an alien scout.

Rzis's not-intended stood in the precise formation behind her commander with four others. He dragged his gaze upwards from her boots, comparing her outfit against her companions'. A uniform, clear as his own for the Protectors'. He hadn't noticed before, had only found the tight material and abundance of outer pockets odd.

His stomach tightened, and he shifted to his largest four-footed form. He hadn't shifted involuntarily since childhood. Unfair that she could still make him surprise himself. Tail dancing in the air, he slunk to the rear of the room and prowled the walls. He refused to escape the situation entirely, unwilling to leave the dignitaries.

"We'll need to discuss your request in diplomatic chambers," a minister said.

Rzis trotted to stand at one of the six exits, shoulder to shoulder with the security lioness at that post. The guard smelled relieved to share the responsibility in the face of all this drama. A high pitched whine sounded *Urgent Notice* in her ear, which Rzis wouldn't have heard if he hadn't been standing so close. Or in Skyline form. She gave Rzis a nod that said *watch this door for me?* and transformed to a body with a voice box so she could duck into the hallway and take her call. It was probably routine.

The Terran commander: "Of course. Take your time. We can adjourn to our ship."

"That won't be necessary," said the same minister as before.

Yes, the councilors knew better than to let them regroup. Well, Rzis intended to cast his vote when the time came for all Skylines to offer opinions. He would do his part to ensure that the duplicitous monsters flew far from Elsajh, never to return.

Maybe not-Zean would want to stay? Too bad. She'd drawn on his affections for too long. He couldn't afford the interest. She could hunt for some other world to swindle.

The guard had been outside for longer than conscionable while on duty. Rzis cocked a rounded ear and focused his hearing outside the chamber. Shouting filtered through the doors and vents, getting closer.

The guard opened the door and stumbled inside, letting in the fugue of war. More shouting, some screams, the sick *thud* of flesh on flesh, the whirring grind of a Shalanite's gruesome weapon warming up.

His tail puffed out. Betrayed already! Rzis roared his warning to the room. The Terrans had ceased pretending and already moved to take the building. This farce was a mere distraction. Did not-Zean know the depths her counterparts plumbed? His lungs shrank and expanded again. Irrelevant.

The Sky People had made Elsajh better for nothing, their work of generations undone in a moment of weakness. *His* weakness. This warning roar came too late. Days too late, with the advance force already in their midst.

This was not the time for anguish. But for *action*.

If he died stopping this takeover. Then he would die.

He roared again, but stayed near the door, ready to take any who would dare to enter. The other Skylines present could deal with the Terran decoys. Still, he kept half an eye on the clump of foreigners. Most Skylines in the room had transformed. The larger ones preparing for battle, the smaller ones huddling together, unsure at this juncture whether to flee or talk.

The Terrans all stayed in two legged forms, even not-Zean, making them easy to spot. All six had hands on their weapons, none out of holsters... yet.

Their leader asked, "You sure about these here people, Mahdan?"

Not-Zean at his back replied, "I'm sure, ma'am. These are the friends we want." Her voice was steady, clear. She had all the qualities you'd want in a comrade-in-arms. Poor luck she was comrades with the invaders.

"All right, then."

The door opened again, a thunderous harbinger. The boundary clamored with anger and pain and the hot humidity of bodies. Bodies that swarmed inward, all merely two legged, but more than enough to overwhelm the six-person honor guard. Every Skyline would have to fight.

Fingers dug into Rzis's fur, and he flipped his assailant to the ground. A dark brown patch fluttered on his winded attacker's linen shirt. Shalanite! How had the Terrans set this up so quickly? Had they watched Elsajh for dissent before sending not-Zean to infiltrate? He nosed at the patch.

Then roared in pain.

Sharp. Hot. Blood ran down his hind leg from a knife's deep stab. A heavy weight draped across his spine. It pressed him down, squeezed at his lungs. Spots, lights. He rolled, trying to dislodge the attacker. A flash of Shalanite brown linen floated in the air. The whining spin of a vaporizer gearing up to attack.

*Bang!*

The weight fell off, and Rzis rolled to the other side, lying on the floor and panting. His eyesight blurry, he could still make out his harrier, dead from a small hole to the heart. Not something any Elsajh weapon could do, though he'd seen its like on the station above. *Projectiles.* He shuffled his head toward the Terrans, ready to make eye contact with not-Zean, his savior. *She really does care for me.* But the Terran pointing a tube in his direction was a tall, burly stranger, more square-than person-shaped.

Rzis's breath sped, even as his heart rate slowed. The Terrans hadn't come to destroy his planet after all. He nodded to his savior. They had no reason to side with the Shalanites, wanted to make friends rather than become some imperialist power. His mistaken intended had said as much, but he hadn't listened.

The doorways swarmed with Shalanite brown now, possibly enough to take down all of Elsajh's elite. Those vaporizers would make them equal to Skyline claws.

*Crack!*

A new weight fell on Rzis's tail, and he pushed it off. Pushed himself up to standing. He would defend this room with everything he had left. With all the blood remaining in his body. For the protectorate. His mouth opened in a greatcat's grin, pointed teeth on display.

This dead body had the same telltale hole, most likely made by a Terran weapon. Perhaps the Terran projectile motion armaments could stand against the Shalanite's vaporizers where sleek muscle and meat-rending teeth could not.

All around the room, Shalanites poured through the entrance points and hit the floor, lives cut short by alien mechanics. Perhaps, if he'd had a Terran-style weapon with its accuracy and speed, he could have caused as much carnage. But perhaps not. War, death on this scale, was as alien to Elsajh as Terran fashion. It had been ever since the Sky People came.

*This is what the Shalanites want to recreate? Our native culture: a world covered in blood.*

A yowling scream, cut off by a Shalanite vaporizer.

The unfortunate victim came apart, and a tangy miasma coated Rzis's tongue. Bellowing cries and the *thump* of rushing paws on the other side of the room.

A Shalanite weapon whirred to readiness close by.

Rzis prowled toward the sound, hunting the vile warmonger who'd penetrated the Terrans' perimeter. Booted feet copied his steps from behind. He saw a flash of pockets. His shadow was Terran. A joint action, then.

From beneath a stack of bodies, the Shalanite laughed and laughed and laughed. His weapon pointed at Rzis and the Terran. "We will end this false oppression. *Hic.* Our people's last stand will be—"

The Terran used his projectile weapon twice in quick succession. It was louder up close. And smelled of smoke. Better that than of blood and death.

The Shalanite fell silent.

Rzis stood still on his three-and-a-half feet, heat radiating from the unnamed ally at his side. He listened, searched. No screams or *bangs* or battle cries. Just panting. Bodies. A Skyline being tended by not-Zean. A dancer crying. But no more deadly whirring.

The Terran commander snapped, "Simpson, Chavez! Check the floor below. Nguyen, start patching up the wounded. Qaitra, coordinate containment." Quieter, she said, "Vasquez, you're with me." The commander was leaning on the man at her side, presumably *Vasquez*.

Not-Zean waved to him, and Rzis shifted to wave back and head her direction. Her people had been amazingly brave. He'd gotten lucky. If they'd truly been the monsters he'd feared... He stumbled on his weak leg.

The Terran at his side eased him down to the floor. "Looks like that went straight into the muscle. Gonna be a sonova to keep from scarring."

Rzis got the gist of that, if not the literal meaning. "It would have been worse without your people here."

Maybe the Terrans were this generation's version of the Sky People.

# Chapter Fourteen

*If our ship flew at the speed of diplomacy, we'd
have died before seeing a single other planet.*
*– Commander Asti Yogifire*

And you were there for everything else, ma'am.

**For the record, Mahdan, please explain the fallout
from your choices and our involvement in this
alien firefight.**

Not so alien anymore, right?

**The consequences of our actions will affect how
our choices are viewed by posterity, yes.**

Ooooh, big words.

**You can use any words you like, short or long, to
*finish off your testimony already*.**

My whole company waited three days on the planet's surface, held off with talk of deliberations *in diplomatic chambers*. Mostly this consisted of the locals having huge meetings to which we weren't invited, punctuated by the commander being called into a large meeting and not telling anyone else what had gone on. Hmmph.

We'd been staying at Zean's parents' home. They had plenty of space, and they saw it as good for their image to host these strangers who had possibly done them wrong. For my part, I enjoyed running through the wildflower garden and smothered the desire to terrorize Zean's obnoxious brothers. Which isn't to say that I wouldn't shift and then lie in wait to confuse one of them who was just coming from seeing his sister. But I refrained from pouncing on them unawares.

Plenty of locals came by to check us out, the curiosities. Well, they really came to gawk at me. Aliens were old hat on this side of the stars, but a new race of Sky People? That was exciting. Not to mention the reporters who didn't believe that Margavi was last week's news. Now that the person they wanted to interview was willing to talk, they were *going* to interview.

One thing really bothered me, though: Rzis hadn't visited. I had no idea what he was doing or what he was thinking. Once, on the second day, Zean teased me about it. "So nice of you to care about *my* marriage prospects." I turned leonine till the next morning, refusing to speak or play with anyone. She didn't say anything about Rzis again.

Now that my identity—and my species—were common knowledge, now that he'd had a chance to think things over, I'd expected to see him. Well, I'd hoped anyway.

On the morning of the fourth day, though, I finally got my wish. I was in the wildflower garden—they had a new teal-colored plant that made me sneeze, but it smelled like oranges and I couldn't stay away—when a plaintive "Mew?" interrupted my sneezing and sniffling.

A dark, sleek cat, tall as my waist, nudged at my hand, forcing me to pet him, but so softly that I barely felt the rush of fur on skin. "I didn't think I'd you'd come." Because this had to be Rzis, my dark lion who was comfortable with my touch but unsure whether he still deserved it. At least, I hoped that was the right interpretation. Nobody had wanted my touch before this planet, and now I was something of a celebrity.

Only blondes and mottled calicos lived in Zean's house. The single dark cat I'd seen at this residence had been my sort-of suitor.

He changed back. "I wasn't sure you'd *want* to see me again." He twisted loose sleeves around his downy wrists. "Not after I—" He dropped his arms and looked me directly in my slitted eyes. "After I abandoned you."

I shrugged with a nonchalance I didn't feel. "At least you didn't arrest me."

"I should have trusted you," he insisted.

And no, no that wasn't right at all. We could both have done many things differently, but he'd already been *too* trusting. I wasn't kidding about the potential arrest. He should've officially questioned me about the person I was impersonating. Should have dragged me into police custody. Should have kept me as bait for my potentially deadly allies. "*Never* apologize for skepticism. *Never*." Earth had learned that lesson the hard way. And it wasn't there anymore. I'd hate for the same to be true of Elsajh, a planet where Baastet's Children would be welcome instead of reviled.

He shrunk from my vehemence, then took a deep breath and launched into what I thought would be a speech. "I know you have responsibilities, but I'd like you to stay." It was a short speech.

No one had ever wanted me to stay before. Anywhere. I almost didn't care what the reason was. Maybe he liked having a friend that was willing to unite annexed buildings. Maybe he wanted the fame of being the guy who knew the new Sky Person before she was revealed. Or maybe this was a romance thing. I knew others of Baastet's Children had to have been involved somewhere along the line—else, where did the kits come from—but that had never really been an issue for me. Or for anyone else I knew.

Deflection was key. "Do you even know my name?"

He gulped and blushed, hotly enough to turn his neck a bright red under the tactile-friendly coat of vellus. Guess these people *did* blush when embarrassed. We had so much in common. "I don't have to know your name," he declared, committed to his course. "I know enough about you. I know that you're smart and strong and care about the people of Elsajh. If it's not too forward of me, I'd like permission to court you, whatever your name is."

I breathed too deeply, nostrils flaring, and sneezed. It was nice to be complimented, if a bit weird. Clearly, this culture had no hang-ups about interspecies relations. I wondered if that came from their obsession with their mysterious Sky People. "My name is Maya," I told him. "And I thought you were courting Zean."

He leaned forward to nudge my cheek with his nose, though both of us were hominid, and I barely kept myself from springing back at this infringement on my personal space. Different planet, different culture. "I've never met Zean, have I? In fact," he whispered conspiratorially, "she stood me up."

His proposition sounded better than good, but the truth of the matter was that I had a job to do. Mahdan Maya Qaitra, *first class*. It'd be years, decades, before I'd do all the work of a Terran Mahdan. I might have some problems with my people, but they were still my people, and I'd still do everything in my power to make sure we continued to live and thrive among these foreign stars. "You know my ship will be leaving soon." And yet, this was the perfect planet for a shapeshifter, and Rzis was the perfect companion I'd never known I wanted—staid and calm, smart and agile. I picked at a trouser thread, avoiding his eyes. "I can't ask, but... would you wait for me?" I asked anyway.

"I..." He paused, then started over. "When I left you at the café, I was so angry. More with myself for not realizing you weren't Zean or one of the Sky People. I'd just given up on Zean, you know, having met her lover." My head came up, and he looked straight into my slit-pupiled eyes with no hesitation. He gave me a trembling smile. "But then you were *there*. And you weren't her, but that was better because I didn't have to concede. But if you weren't Zean, what did that mean? Would you disappear the way you arrived, unheralded and unknown?" He offered me his hands to hold, extending them to rest on my legs, the reverse of what we'd done that day in the tree.

I put my hands into his completely and shifted them to paws, proof to Terrans of my purpose: traveling the stars to sniff out biologically compatible species. It was a reminder to myself.

He jerked back, mesmerized by my partial shift. I guessed that wasn't a standard thing on this planet. He breathed a curse, but then returned to tighten his grip on my squared wrists. "I realized I couldn't bear it if you disappeared."

Oh. That. That was. Wow.

I changed my paws to hands and laced our fingers. We sat among the wildflowers for the rest of the morning. Together.

Come afternoon, a diplomatic gopher came to link with the commander. "Miss, um, Baastet?" he called to me. Someone had told the diplomats that Terran lions were called *Baastet's Children* and no one had been willing to acknowledge my family name of *Qaitra* since. "They request your attendance in chambers. If it's not too much trouble." This planet was kind of weird. There was no reason for this guy to be so nervous around me. In my hominid form, I'm not all that intimidating.

Nothing for it. I left Rzis in the garden and joined the commander in diplomatic chambers.

"This is much more crowded than I've seen it," she whispered to me when we entered a room full of bodies and chairs and desks, arranged in a circle with a raised platform in the center. "They must've reached a decision."

A housecat broke from the chairs and sway-walked toward the platform as soon as the doors had closed behind us. It shifted to become a woman—maybe sixty years old or so, by Terran reckoning of age—who ascended the two steps to speaker's position.

"Ladies and gentlemen of Elsajh, Terran visitors, friends, Sky People," she addressed all the important groups in her audience. "It is a strange topic we decide here today. So strange that not everything can be decided at once.

"We have long been citizens of the galaxy, not simply of our cities or our planet. This makes one decision clear and simple: the Terran diplomats and scientists are welcome to talk and study among us, provided they fill out the standard paperwork. We hope that the spirit of cooperation is mirrored by our Terran friends and that we will learn as much from them as they from us."

That covered all the objectives of a first contact. Say what you like about Baastet's Children, we have a special job, and I am amazing at that job. Still only first class, and my record's a jillion times better than my ship's previous Mahdan's. Because I'm amazing. Did I mention the amazingness of me? Anyway, since I'd found us this compatible planet and gotten us a bunch of handy contacts, we could start importing passengers. Scientists and statesmen, mostly. We had a bunch in residence on the boat upstairs.

Of course, that meant we were done down here. My fingers went cold, and I shifted them into paws, but that didn't help. It wasn't a physical chill. I'd miss this place. I'd miss the freedom to walk around leonine, unbothered. I'd miss the way strangers helped each other. I'd even miss the fur-matting dust.

My shoulders hunched up to hide my neck, and I sighed.

I'd miss Rzis, my first leonine friend since training days. My first beloved.

"But there is more to this meeting," the woman continued. And from here she told the story of my duplicitous arrival—a word that made me cringe—and heroic exploits. Then she offered the choice of what to do with me... to Zean's family. Their options:

(1) press charges for impersonating a family member

(2) have my species (Baastet's Children, not Terrans) permanently tossed off the planet

(3) other, at their discretion

A graying lynx switched places with the woman on the platform and transformed into Zean's father's hominid form. "We, the family, are grateful for this chance to address this issue." He smiled at me. "We are very happy to welcome Mahdan Maya Baastet and her brethren to our home. It has been a long time since Elsajh has seen the courage of the Sky People in person. Our lost brothers and sisters of Terra are welcome here."

My breath whooshed out of me, and I smiled so hugely that my commander sidled away. No executions! My heart beat faster as the adrenaline pumped all through my veins with no fear to fuel.

Zean's father wasn't finished. "As a gesture of goodwill to all the people of Earth and to all of Baastet's Children, we would like to adopt Maya into our family." He addressed me directly. "You've already been a member of our family for days, showing your nobility and respect for our name. We would be honored to have you join us in truth."

*Family!* Someone wanted to claim me. My stomach tightened, and a small laugh punched out of me. At least, I think it was a laugh. Hysteria, maybe? This was all too much. I looked to my wide-eyed commander who nodded furiously. She motioned me to go go *go*.

"Yes," I said, my voice shaking. This was whole new territory.

*It can't last. You'll have to leave, Mahdan.* I bit my lip and curled inwards. Sure, the commander wanted me to cement good relations with the locals, but that didn't mean I'd get to stay. I shrugged to knock myself out of the spiral. I should enjoy this feeling of *belonging* while I could. My shipmates would trample over it soon enough.

"Then, would Maya *Skyline* please join me on the stand?"

And that was it. Easy as easy can be on this world. Want to adopt someone, just get their permission. So long as I didn't have to do any paperwork, I wasn't complaining. Way this was going, I'd be very welcome here whenever my tour was up. The moment I made Mahdan S-class, I was quitting the Terran service and coming here. I could do more good for the Terran cause by raising the next generation.

A shiny black cub came forward and batted at my feet, motioning for me to make some space, but not leave the platform. Rzis transformed and spoke to Zean's—my!—father in a voice loud enough to reverberate in the rafters. "Sir," he said, "I have been your Chosen to marry your daughter for months. Now that you have two daughters, I petition to court the eldest."

My new father questioned me with his eyes, and I nodded again. I supposed Rzis could travel with me if he wanted, so long as the commander didn't object, just until I made S-class and had the seniority to leave for my new home planet. I'd always be Terran, but I was an *Elsajh*-Terran.

Rzis nuzzled my neck and both my cheeks for all the newscasters to see.

Father addressed the assembly again. "We have here the perfect chance to cement the relations among all these parties. Elsajh, Terran, Sky People, Baastet's Children. What treaty is more sacred to all peoples than this? Elsajh Rzis Skyline and Terran Maya Qaitra Baastet-Skyline shall be wed before her Terran companions leave our world."

*Whoa. What?* Applause and cheering broke out from the diplomats, and I heard Simpson whistling, "Green grass and a coooooool man, kitty-cat."

As we stepped down from the platform, my new father whispered to me. "Thank the Sky People we have you. Who knows what Zean is thinking? At least she can be the delinquent daughter now without causing problems for the rest of us. We've been trying to unite her with Rzis for ages."

I grinned at him. "I know," I whispered. "Maybe she should meet him sometime."

He gasped, and I knew he'd been in the dark about just how long I'd been impersonating his daughter.

> **Into the record, I submit this recording of Mahdan Qaitra-Baastet-Skyline's testimony as well as a transcript thereof. The file will also contain attendant depositions from myself and from the aliens involved. I, Commander Asti Yogifire, hereby declare this inquiry closed.**

And my viable-colony streak is still a million times better than your *last* Mahdan's.

> **Though it may be coming to an end.**

Aww, c'mon. I'm brilliant at this. You know it. You love me. And since my new father managed to lengthen my betrothal instead of making me get married right away, I'm still free to work for you in every planet's eyes.

> **Don't push it. And I meant that I'm assigning you as Special Envoy to Elsajh until the appointed ambassador arrives with the next wave of "visiting cultural exchange specialists."**

That won't take *that* long.

> These people like you. Because of you, they're let-
> ting us lease whole buildings before we can prove
> Terrans have the money to pay the rent. Odds are
> good the ambassador's going to want to keep you
> around, maybe permanently.

It's a good thing I like planets.

THE END

If you liked this novella for its fun comedy elements, you may be interested in

# Cracked!

## A Magic iPhone Story

*"Cracked! is kind of my new favorite thing in the world... zany and off-kilter"* – *Taryn Albright, The Girl With the Green Pen*

**What can your phone do for you?**

This is the story of a girl and her iPhone. No, that's not quite right. This is the story of a middle-aged statistician and her best friend. Though she didn't consider herself middle-aged. And the best friend was more of a roommate-with-whom-she'd-developed-a-friendship. And this description completely ignores the 6,000-year-old elf with whom the woman and her best friend enjoyed story gaming.

*So let's try this again.*

This is the story of a woman who wished to find love, but who would rather play story games than actively look for it. Especially in the wake of a horrid break-up six months before from a man who had never sent her a single gift.

Until this Valentine's Day, when she received a brand new iPhone in a box with his name on it.

Between story gaming and succumbing to the phone's insidious sleekness, she learns that friendship trumps romance.

In *Cracked! A Magic iPhone Story*, award-winning author Janine A. Southard (a Seattle denizen) shows you how the geeks of Seattle live, provides a running and often-hilarious social commentary on today's world, and reminds you that, so long as you have friends, you are never alone.

If you liked this novella for its space opera roots, you may be interested in The Hive Queen Saga

# Queen & Commander

Winner of the Independent Book Publisher's Award for Science Fiction (2013)

**Do your Test results define you?** Teens flee their Test results in a not-quite-stolen spaceship that they can't fly. An ensemble adventure with intrigue, science, and deception.

> *"...everything I love about science fiction"*
> *– Donnie Darko Girl review blog*

On a world where high school test scores determine your future, six students rebel. They'll outrun society as fast as their questionably obtained spaceship will take them.

**Rhiannon** doesn't technically cheat the Test. She's smarter than the computers that administer it, and she uses that to her advantage. She emerges from Test Day with the most prestigious career possible: **Hive Queen**.

**Gwyn & Victor** are madly in love, but their Test results will tear them apart. Good thing Rhiannon is Gwyn's best friend. Rhiannon can fix this. Queens can do anything.

**Gavin** is the wild card. Raised off-planet, he can't wait to leave again... and he's heard of an empty ship in orbit. The *Ceridwen's Cauldron*.

**Spaceships. Blackmail. Anywhere but here.**

*"Right from the beginning I was trying to figure out the intricacies."*
*– Pagan Book Reviews*

*"...like Joss Whedon's Firefly but for teenagers."*
*– The YA's Nightstand*

**Find these books
and more by Janine A. Southard
at major online booksellers.**

**Or ask your local bookstore to order you a copy!**

# About the Author

Janine A. Southard is the IPPY-award-winning author of *Queen & Commander* (and other books in The Hive Queen Saga). She lives in Seattle, WA, where she writes speculative fiction and reads it aloud to her cat.

The cat appreciates all of these things. Maybe.

To get a free short story and stay up-to-date with her releases, sales, and appearances, join her mailing list. http://bit.ly/janinenews

Visit her on the Web: http://www.janinesouthard.com
Interact on Twitter: http://www.twitter.com/jani_s